MURDER IN THE BASEMENT

MURDER IN THE BASEMENT

ANTHONY BERKELEY

With an Introduction by
Martin Edwards

Introduction © 2021, 2023 by Martin Edwards
Murder in the Basement © 1932 by The Estate of Anthony Berkeley Cox
Cover and internal design © 2023 by Sourcebooks
Front cover image © NRM/Pictorial Collection/Science & Society Picture Library

Published by Poisoned Pen Press, an imprint of Sourcebooks,
in association with the British Library
P.O. Box 4410, Naperville, Illinois 60567-4410
(630) 961-3900
sourcebooks.com

Originally published in 1932 by Hodder & Stoughton, London.

Library of Congress Cataloging-in-Publication Data

Names: Berkeley, Anthony, author. | Edwards, Martin, writer of introduction.
Title: Murder in the basement / Anthony Berkeley ;
with an introduction by Martin Edwards.
Description: Naperville, Illinois : Poisoned Pen Press,
[2022] | Series: British Library Crime Classics
Identifiers: LCCN 2022006673 (print) | LCCN 2022006674
(ebook) | (trade paperback) | (epub)
Classification: LCC PR6005.O855 M87 2022 (print) | LCC
PR6005.O855 (ebook) | DDC 823/.912--dc23
LC record available at https://lccn.loc.gov/2022006673
LC ebook record available at https://lccn.loc.gov/2022006674

Printed and bound in the United States of America.
SB 10 9 8 7 6 5 4 3 2

CONTENTS

INTRODUCTION

Murder in the Basement was published in 1932, at a time when the author, whose full name was Anthony Berkeley Cox, had reached the height of his powers. Writing as Anthony Berkeley, he had established himself as one of the leading detective novelists of his generation. In the same year that this book appeared, he also published his second outstanding novel of psychological suspense, wholly different in content and style from this Berkeley novel. *Before the Fact* was published under another pen-name, Francis Iles, and later filmed by Alfred Hitchcock as *Suspicion*.

In *Murder in the Basement*, not for the first time, Berkeley broke fresh ground as a crime writer. At the time the novel appeared, however, its pioneering nature was not recognised. Indeed, the book received rather less acclaim than much of his other work, and over the years it has received little critical attention. This is no doubt because Berkeley's customary wit and ingenuity are less in evidence than in novels such as his masterpiece, *The Poisoned Chocolates Case*, which has also been reprinted as a British Library Crime Classic. The mood is low-key and Roger Sheringham, that most opinionated of amateur sleuths, is off-stage for much of the time; even when he does turn up, his manner is rather less ebullient than usual.

Yet although at first sight *Murder in the Basement* might seem to lack the characteristic zest of the more renowned Sheringham novels, on closer examination it offers a very good example of Berkeley's admirable determination to keep trying to do something fresh with the crime story.

In the prologue, a newly married couple return from their honeymoon to their new home in Lewisham only to discover human remains buried in the basement. Chief Inspector Moresby of Scotland Yard begins to investigate and quickly establishes two crucial facts. The corpse belongs to a woman, and she has been shot through the back of the head. But who was she? Identifying the deceased proves exceptionally difficult. The first major section of the novel is devoted to painstaking police work, with an emphasis on forensic detection, until Moresby ascertains the dead woman's identity, and that she worked at a preparatory school called Roland House.

Moresby recalls that, by happy coincidence, his friend Sheringham has recently deputised for a master at Roland House in order to collect "local colour" for a novel he planned to write. He wrote a few chapters before abandoning the manuscript, having based the characters on the people he met at the school. Moresby, who likes to amuse himself at Sheringham's expense, invites him to use his deductive powers to work out the victim's identity from the manuscript. And that manuscript forms the next part of the book. It is, in effect, an extended flashback which presents the principal characters at the school and the tensions in their relationships.

This was, as far as I know, the first detective novel to contain a "whowasdunin" mystery. That is, the detective—and the reader—are challenged to determine from the information presented which member of a group of people is the murder victim.

The "whowasdunin" mystery is not the be-all and end-all of *Murder in the Basement*. The solution to this particular puzzle is revealed at the start of the third main part of the book. Two threads of the narrative still need to be resolved. First, who is the killer? Second, will it prove possible to bring the culprit to justice? Will patient police work prevail, or will Sheringham's enthusiasm for psychology enable him to steal a march on Moresby? As further information comes to light, the answers to these questions appear to be predictable, but it is worth bearing in mind that Anthony Berkeley delighted in confounding expectations.

One or two other Golden Age writers, including Britain's Leo Bruce and the American Anita Boutell, subsequently wrote "whowasdunin" mysteries, but this type of writing is more commonly associated with another American author, Patricia McGerr, whose 1946 debut *Pick Your Victim* is an enjoyable example of the form. Two very successful post-war novels which have appeared in the Crime Classics series, Julian Symons's *The Colour of Murder* and Mary Kelly's *The Spoilt Kill*, also offer "whowasdunin" puzzles, while in recent times Lucy Foley's bestsellers *The Hunting Party* and *The Guest List* show that this type of mystery has enduring appeal. But it was Berkeley who led the way.

Anthony Berkeley Cox (1893–1971) was educated at Sherborne School and University College, Oxford, and served in the army during the First World War; during the conflict, he was gassed, and his health never fully recovered. When peace came, he turned to journalism and was a regular contributor to *Punch*. His first detective novel, *The Layton Court Mystery*, appeared in 1925, and introduced Sheringham. This book, and its successor, *The Wychford Poisoning Case*, were at first published anonymously, and throughout his life he guarded his privacy jealously.

In 1928, he hosted a dinner for fellow detective novelists which was such a success that further such dinners followed, and he was inspired to found the Detection Club in 1930; it thrives to this day. By the time the club adopted formal rules and a constitution (in the same year that *Murder in the Basement* was published), it had established itself as an elite social club for the genre's most prominent British writers.

There is an entertaining exchange between Moresby and Sheringham in this novel, when the policeman says:

"You mean, you used the real people there for your book?"

"Well, of course. One always does that, in spite of the law of libel and the funny little notices some people put in the front of their books to say that all the characters in the story are imaginary. Imaginary my hat! Nobody could imagine a character and make it live."

Sheringham (who himself represented one aspect of his creator's complex personality) was undoubtedly speaking for Berkeley, whose books are crammed with people who are thinly disguised versions of those he knew. One wonders if this technique helps to explain why Berkeley eventually ran out of steam as a novelist. His career effectively came to an end following the indifferent reception of the third Francis Iles novel, *As for the Woman,* which was published in 1939. Thereafter he wrote a few short stories but the creative spark was gone. He became known primarily as an extremely perceptive critic of the genre under the Iles name. Among the many emerging writers whose gifts he was quick to recognise were P. D. James and Ruth Rendell.

Berkeley's cynicism and love of irony are much in evidence in *Murder in the Basement,* and so is his flair for taking the genre in new directions. He is a writer of major importance in the history of crime fiction and this undeservedly underestimated novel is an interesting example of his unorthodox approach to his craft.

—Martin Edwards
www.martinedwardsbooks.com

A NOTE FROM THE PUBLISHER

The original novels and short stories reprinted in the British Library Crime Classics series were written and published in a period ranging, for the most part, from the 1890s to the 1960s. There are many elements of these stories which continue to entertain modern readers; however, in some cases there are also uses of language, instances of stereotyping, and some attitudes expressed by narrators or characters that may not be endorsed by the publishing standards of today. We acknowledge therefore that some elements in the works selected for reprinting may continue to make uncomfortable reading for some of our audience. With this series British Library Publishing and Poisoned Pen Press aim to offer a new readership a chance to read some of the rare books of the British Library's collections in an affordable paperback format, to enjoy their merits, and to look back into the world of the twentieth century as portrayed by its writers. It is not possible to separate these stories from the history of their writing and as such the following novel is presented as it was originally published with minor edits only, made for consistency of style and sense. We welcome feedback from our readers.

TO
GLYNN and NANCY

PROLOGUE

Young Mr. Reginald Dane drew his wife into a corner of the higgledy-piggledy drawing-room.

"I say," he whispered, with a cautious eye on the hall. "I say, darling, how much do you think I ought to give these men?"

"Haven't the least idea, darling," Molly Dane whispered back. "Ten shillings, would you think?"

"Between the three of them?" Reginald whispered doubtfully. "Better spring a quid, hadn't I? They get pretty big tips, these chaps."

"That ought to be plenty."

Young Mr. Dane nodded in a conspirator-like way and, emerging from the corner, walked with an air of extreme carelessness towards a large man with a walrus moustache, who was hovering in an intent manner just inside the open front door. The large man affected to start in astonishment at perceiving Reginald approaching him.

"Think you'll find everything quite satisfactory now, sir," said the large man, very deferentially.

Reginald nodded. He did not say that, to his certain knowledge, every single article of furniture, so carefully labelled in advance with the name of the room for which it was destined, had been put in a wrong one, so that he and Molly would have to spend several laborious hours in sorting them out. Young Mr. Dane was not one to make unnecessary fuss. He simply said:

"Oh, yes. Quite. Most satisfactory. Perfectly. Excellent. Er—here you are."

A look of bland amazement passed over the walrus moustache as its owner caught sight of Reginald's outstretched hand.

"Well, thank you, sir," he said, in tones of great wonder. "Thank you kindly."

"That's for—er—that's among the three of you, you know."

"Oh, yes, sir. Very good of you, I'm sure."

"Not at all," said Reginald, and fled.

"Was it enough?" asked his wife anxiously, as he rejoined her in the little drawing-room.

"Oh, yes, I think so," Reginald replied nonchalantly. "He seemed quite pleased."

Side by side they peeped through the uncurtained window.

With much banging and clattering the three men were closing up the end of the big furniture-van. One took his place at the wheel, one got up beside him, the third climbed into the back, and with a rapt, thirsty look on their faces the three emissaries of Ate drove away. If ever Ate returned to earth it would surely be in the guise of a furniture-remover. There is something so fateful about a furniture-van. Relentlessness urges it forward, and Destiny sits at the wheel.

Mr. Reginald Dane slipped an arm about his wife's waist. "Well, darling, here we are," he observed.

"We are, darling," his wife agreed.

"Sorry the honeymoon's over, and all that?"

His wife smiled, and shook her head.

Looking down into her smiling, upturned face, young Mr. Dane saw that it was good. He kissed it.

"So now let's go and look round all this semi-detached messuage or tenement known to men as 4, Burnt Oak Road, Lewisham, in the county of Middlesex," said Reginald, quoting, somewhat inaccurately, from memory.

With solemn steps as befitted such a ceremonial, their arms about each other's waists, Mr. and Mrs. Dane made their state progress from room to room. And wherever they looked, in spite of the disorder, in spite of the furniture so wrongly disposed, in spite of a wicked scratch on the brand-new dining-room table—lo! it was good.

Then Molly went off to make some tea in their new kitchen, and Reginald wandered in the direction of the front door. He opened it and planted himself in the little porch outside, and his eyes travelled proudly over the tiny strip of front garden at his feet. After that he went and planted himself in the French windows that opened out of the dining-room at the back and surveyed the minute garden there, with its pocket-handkerchief lawn and its ragged little beds, now flowerless whatever had once been in them, for the month was the depressing one of January. But to Reginald it was more beautiful than Kew in June.

"There's even a cellar, you remember," chanted Reginald, now at the kitchen door. "I'm going to have a look at it."

Molly, busy with buttered toast, nodded brightly. "Don't get too dirty, darling. Hadn't you better wait till after tea? Why not see if you can get some of the curtains up now?"

"Curtains!" said Reginald with scorn. "When there might be a chest of gold forgotten in the cellar. You never know what people may leave behind. Darling, you must see that I couldn't possibly have tea till I know for certain whether there's a chest of gold in the cellar or not."

He opened the door under the stairs, and ran down the flight of narrow steps.

It was not a large cellar, certainly, but then it is something to have a cellar at all in a semi-detached villa in the suburbs. Moreover this particular cellar was lit by electric light. Reginald turned the switch and regarded the eight-by-ten cell of whitewashed brick with high approval; even the cobwebs, hanging in thick festoons from every available projection, seemed to him the most satisfactory cobwebs he had ever seen. Draped round a bottle of old port, for instance...

In a moment Reginald had furnished the whole cellar with row upon row of delectable bottles.

Well, it really would make a perfect wine-cellar. The temperature was just about right, and the air seemed dry. The lime-wash on the walls was firm and hard, and the brick floor showed no signs of dampness. Except perhaps in one corner; the corner remote from the entrance. Reginald went across to look at it.

Certainly that corner was a little curious. There was a slight depression in the floor there—a long, narrow depression, about five feet by fifteen inches, where the bricks seemed to have been laid not quite so evenly as over the rest of the floor. Reginald kicked the projecting edge of one idly, but it was quite firm.

Then something else caught his eye. Elsewhere, the floor was frankly dirty, with a fine, dark-grey dust; but near one end of the depression, more towards the centre of the cellar, was a round patch of quite different colour, a light grey, through which the redness of the bricks did not show as it did on the rest of the floor. With sudden interest Reginald bent down and examined it.

Then he whistled, and began to look at the remainder of the floor with intentness. As if suddenly, and quite unexpectedly, finding something that he was looking for, he bent down again and ran his hand once or twice over some bricks in the very middle of the floor, examining the result on his finger-tips. Finally, with a loud whoop, he bounded up the cellar steps and into the kitchen.

"I've found it, darling! I've found our chest of gold!"

Molly, pouring boiling water into the tea-pot, looked up. "*What?*"

"Well, perhaps it mayn't be a chest of gold, but it's something. Someone's been hiding something in the cellar, under the floor, and bricked it up again. Come and look."

"But the toast will get cold."

"Blow the toast! Put it under the grid. Darling, you *must* come."

Molly came.

In the cellar Reginald proudly explained. "See that depression? That's where it is. And see that light-coloured patch? That's where they mixed the mortar to cement the bricks in again. Must be. And see this patch just here? Look—it's earth! Someone had those bricks up not so long ago, dug a hole underneath, piled the earth here, and cached something. When he put the earth back again he didn't stamp it down tight enough, and it's sunk; hence that depression. Darling, I'm convinced there's a chest of gold under this floor."

"Much more likely to have been a plumber, playing with the drains," replied Mrs. Dane, who was a matter-of-fact young woman.

"Anyhow, I'm going to see. I noticed a rusty old pickaxe in the garden. I'm going to have those bricks up." He bounded up the stairs again.

"But, darling, tea's ready," wailed his wife after him.

Reginald carried out his excavations alone. Not all the chests of gold in the world can dash a cup of tea from a woman's lips.

Sipping contentedly in the higgledy-piggledy drawing-room, Molly listened to the blows of the pickaxe, and smiled secretly. After a while they ceased, but Reginald did not appear. At last she went to the top of the cellar stairs and called to him.

"Well, darling, is it a chest of gold?"

Her husband's voice came up to her, oddly shaky.

"Don't come down, Molly. There—there's something pretty beastly here. I must get a policeman."

PART I

CHAPTER I

By half-past six the remainder of the bricks and covering earth had been removed by the two constables, with their pickaxes and spades, and the body was fully exposed. Under the directions of the police surgeon it was lifted out of the shallow grave and laid on the floor of the cellar.

"There's no need for your men to stay here," Chief Inspector Moresby told the divisional inspector, for the atmosphere in the cellar was close. "They can wait upstairs, or in the garden."

Thankfully the two lumbered up the cellar stairs with their tools.

"You'd all better go upstairs," grunted the police surgeon as he bent to examine the body. "It's none too pleasant here."

"Well, we can't do any good watching you, doctor, and that's a fact," assented Chief Inspector Moresby. "Come on, both of you."

He led the way out of the cellar, and Sergeant Afford, whom Moresby had brought with him from headquarters, and Inspector Fox followed him.

Young Mr. and Mrs. Dane were hovering anxiously in the hall.

"Is it—is there someone really there?" quavered the latter.

The chief inspector laid a large and kindly hand on the shoulder of each. "It's a bad business, I'm afraid; I won't disguise it from you. About as bad as it can be."

"A nice end to a honeymoon," said young Mr. Dane, with a rather shaky laugh. "What is it, inspector?"

"It's a woman."

"Oh-h-h-h-h," Molly Dane shuddered.

The chief inspector became practical. "Just moved in, haven't you? Now I'm going to make a suggestion. You're not straight here yet, I see; carpets not down and so on. Is there somewhere you could go to for a night or two—friends perhaps, who could put you up? We shall be in and out of here for a day or two, you see, and it won't be very nice for you; then you can come back when we've finished—and I'll get one of my men to give you a hand with your carpets and so on. What do you say? Is it a bargain?"

"I don't feel I could ever come back," said Molly.

"We could go to my wife's people," Reginald replied. "They live in London. And our suit-cases aren't even unpacked yet."

"Then that's arranged," beamed the chief inspector. "I'll send my sergeant round with you in the car, to explain. That's fine. Now, what about those suit-cases? No point in delaying."

Within ten minutes Mr. and Mrs. Dane had set off in a police car on the long ride from Lewisham to Hampstead, escorted, quite unnecessarily Mr. Dane felt, by Sergeant Afford. But then Mr. Dane did not know that the sergeant's real mission was to explain not so much to Mrs. Dane's people as to the local detective division, and add the request that a quiet eye be kept upon the pair while they were in Hampstead. Scotland Yard cannot afford to take anything or anybody at its appearance-value.

In the meantime Chief Inspector Moresby was talking, in the higgledy-piggledy drawing-room, to a stout man with a face like a very gloomy full moon. This was Superintendent Green, from Scotland Yard, who had arrived just as the Danes were leaving.

"About six inches deep, she was. The earth had been packed over her, and the bricks laid again over that. You'll see for yourself, Mr. Green."

"Nude, you say?"

"Except for her gloves. I'd say she was dressed in outdoor things, and the clothes were taken away to prevent identification. The murderer just didn't bother about her gloves."

Green nodded. "That's probably it. Not going to make our job any easier. It's not likely we'll get anything from the gloves, especially as he left them."

"There'll probably be some distinguishing marks on the body, sir," Moresby opined. "Ah, here's Dr. Remington. This is Superintendent Green, doctor, from headquarters. Well? Have you found anything to help us?"

The doctor, a tall, sparse man with a stoop, carefully shut the door behind him. "Not much, I'm afraid, Chief Inspector. The body's in an advanced stage of decomposition, as no doubt you saw. The features certainly aren't recognisable. I'd say she's been buried there for six months at the least."

The two police officers looked glum. Six months meant a very cold trail to be followed.

"Age?" asked Superintendent Green laconically.

"I can't put it nearer than that she was a young, or comparatively young, woman. Say twenty-three to thirty. Well nourished. Healthy, so far as I can see superficially. Teeth in good condition."

"No stoppings?"

"Not one."

The superintendent frowned. Dentists' work is one of the surest ways of identifying an unknown corpse. "What class would you put her in?"

"There again I can hardly tell you. The hands are too far gone to enable me to say whether she was accustomed to work with them, but her gloves look good. I took them off, by the way. I expected you'd want them at once. They're very much stained, but they're all there is in the way of an external clue."

"Thanks. Yes, we'll want to get to work on them at once. She was shot, the chief inspector tells me?"

"Through the back of the head," nodded the doctor. "The bullet passed through, and came out of the forehead."

"Ah! We'll have to find that bullet, Moresby."

"I had a bit of a look round, as soon as we saw she'd been shot," Moresby said dubiously. "I haven't found it yet."

"Any idea of the calibre, doctor?"

"Fairly large, I think. At a guess, and as near as I can put it at present, I should suggest a .45 service revolver."

The detectives looked still more gloomy. So many officers retained their service revolvers after the war, and omitted to take out licences for them, that to trace a shot from one of them, even given the bullet with its distinctive markings, is almost impossible; and when the bullet is missing…

"Any birthmarks, or scars on the body?" asked the superintendent.

"So far as I've been able to see yet, neither. If there were, I doubt if they would still be decipherable. There's not much skin left, you know."

"This looks as if it is going to be a job," grumbled Moresby.

"Too early for the doctor to say yet," Superintendent Green remarked. "We must wait till we've got your full report, Doctor. Can you wait a few minutes? I'll go down with the chief inspector and have a look at the body, and then we'll get it along to the mortuary at once. Ready, Moresby?"

The two detectives went down to the cellar on their gruesome mission.

In the dining-room the divisional inspector and his sergeant had begun a painstaking search of the house, not really with the expectation of finding anything to throw light on the tragedy, but simply because nothing must be left to chance. The two constables were still thankfully inhaling fresh air in the front garden, chatting with their colleague at the gate, whose orders were to admit no one.

A very few minutes sufficed the superintendent for his examination of the body, and he learned from it nothing at all. A rough shroud was then fashioned out of bits of felt and brown paper left by the furniture-removers, and arrangements put in hand for getting it to the mortuary.

"Phew!" said the chief inspector, as he descended again to the cellar with the superintendent. "That's a bit better. Now we can look round properly. You think she was shot here, Mr. Green?"

"Too early to think anything," grunted the other. "Let's see what we can find. The grave first."

The two stout men went down on their knees by the churned-up earth, in the middle of which the impression made by the body was still plain, and began to sift it through their fingers with the utmost care, in search of any article however trifling that might have been inadvertently buried at the same time. When this had proved useless, Moresby took a pick and loosened the surface on which the body had lain, which was also treated in the same way, and finally dug a foot down until he struck a layer of gravel which had plainly never been disturbed. Not so much as a match-stalk rewarded his work.

"Try the walls, then," said the superintendent philosophically.

Here better luck awaited them. On one of the two walls allotted to him Moresby almost at once found a mark on the whitewashed surface, at about the level of his own shoulders, which he examined closely.

"She was shot here, sir. Here's the mark where the bullet struck. Plain traces of lead."

The superintendent came over to look. "Yes, that was no nickel-coated bullet. Bears out what the doctor said. Well…" As if at a command both heads bent abruptly to the floor at the foot of the wall, and simultaneously a disappointed expression appeared on each face. "Not a hope," said Green, voicing their common thought. "He must have taken it off with him. Seems to me we're dealing with a very well-planned crime here, Moresby."

"True enough, Mr. Green," agreed Moresby ruefully, and did not add his fear that the chances of catching its author seemed a little slim.

The two spent another twenty minutes in the cellar, during which every square inch of the walls, ceiling, and floor underwent the scrutiny of at least one pair of keen eyes, without however revealing anything else of the slightest help. All that was plain was that the murderer had shot his victim here, had dug her grave, and had methodically mixed the mortar which he must have expected would hold her down for ever.

Up in the drawing-room again the superintendent lowered his bulk into one of the still-swathed armchairs. "Premeditated, of course," he began to deliver his opinion. "Otherwise why take her into a cellar at all? Dare say he had the cement and sand all ready. Might get a line there. Cement isn't usually bought in small quantities; enquire for a single bag sold six to nine months ago. Sand not so hopeful, but try it all the same. Know anything about this house? Was it empty six months ago?"

"I don't know yet. I thought of having a word with the neighbours on each side as soon as we're through here; and Afford can get on to the house-agent when he gets back. I've got his name and address here. His office will be shut, of course, but Afford can follow him up."

The superintendent nodded approval of these suggestions. "As for the girl, there seemed enough of her face left for the doctors to fake up quite a fair reconstruction," he said grimly. "We'll have that circulated to the Press, of course. And then you'll simply have to work through the 'missing' list; you ought to be able to get a line on her that way, with any luck."

"Yes, sir; of course," said Moresby, without quite so much of his usual geniality. It was an arduous task that his superior officer had tossed him so casually.

"And put Afford on to making enquiries round here. There should be gossip of some kind. That's all I can suggest for the moment. We'll go into it more closely to-morrow morning, when we've got the doctor's report. I'll be getting along now."

When the superintendent had gone, Moresby joined the divisional inspector, who was now ferreting about in the kitchen. The latter reported that so far he had found nothing. "And don't expect to, Mr. Moresby," he added gloomily.

"You never know," Moresby comforted. "And if there is anything, you'll find it, I'm sure. Pay particular attention to the fire-places; that's where people throw things, you know."

It was now getting on for eight o'clock, and as cold as a late January night at that hour might be expected to be. Moresby was not sorry that his own immediate business took him out of the chilly, untenanted house into warmer ones. He stepped into the dank darkness outside, and turned to his left. Burnt Oak Road was made up of pairs of semi-detached villas, of the four-bed., two-sit., spacious-and-commodious-kit., type. The one to which Moresby now turned was the Siamese twin of the Danes'.

A gaping little maid opened the door to him.

"Is Mr. Peters in?" said Moresby pleasantly.

The maid gaped a little wider. "Peters? He don't live here. It's Mr. Cottington as lives here."

"Did I say Peters? I meant Cottington, of course. Is he in?"

"Well, he's having his supper."

One of the doors opening on to the tiny hall was pushed ajar, and a bald little head came round it, to be followed the next moment into the hall by its owner. "Someone to see me, Mabel?"

"Yes, sir, but I told him you was having your supper."

"I've finished, I've finished."

"Then in that case if I might have a word with you, sir," said Moresby, who by this time was inside the hall too.

Mr. Cottington seemed doubtful as to whether his visitor might have a word with him or not. He took off his gold-rimmed spectacles, looked at them dubiously, as if they were an oracle of some sort, and replaced them. "Well..." he said feebly. "I'm rather busy, you know."

"I'm not connected with any business firm, sir," Moresby smiled.

Mr. Cottington brightened. "Oh, well, then. All right. Mabel, you can go. Come into the sitting-room, Mr...?"

"Moresby, sir." The chief inspector became aware of another head round the same door, a rather nice head with greying hair and a comfortably motherly face, at the moment undisguisedly curious. "And if Mrs. Cottington could join us...?"

The next minute they were all three in the sitting-room, sitting comfortably on chairs round a cheerful little fire.

"I didn't wish to say so in front of your maid, Mr. Cottington," Moresby said genially, "but I am a police officer." He produced a card and gave it to his host, who read it with high interest and passed it to his wife.

"Well, really," said that lady, not without trepidation.

"I'm making enquiries about the house next door, No. 4," Moresby explained quickly. "I understand—"

"Oh, what *has* been happening?" interrupted Mrs. Cottington, her trepidation quite forgotten. "I saw the new tenants moving in this afternoon, and the furniture men go away, and I was just wondering whether I'd go across and offer them some tea here, what with them being in such a muddle, when I saw Mr. Dane (I think their name's Dane) run out without his hat or anything, and come back with a policeman; and then more police arrived, and all sorts of other men, and cars, and then Mr. and Mrs. Dane came out to one of the cars and drove off, and the police stayed there. I've just been telling my husband all about it at supper. Mabel— that's our maid—said they've found a body in the cellar, but I couldn't believe that."

The chief inspector sighed behind his smile. At every supper-table in Burnt Oak Road at that very moment, he knew, excited wives were telling incredulous husbands that a body had been found in the cellar at No. 4; and in each case the information would have come from the Mabel of the household.

"Not in this road," added Mr. Cottington. "Always been very quiet and respectable, this road has. That's why we came here ourselves. I told my wife such a thing couldn't happen here. Of course, it's all a silly tale?" Behind their spectacles his eyes gleamed almost as eager a curiosity as his wife's.

Moresby had already made up his mind. A little confidence will produce far greater results in the way of information than a too correct reticence; and in any case the papers had it already. "Yes, it's quite true," he nodded.

"Well, I *never*!" ejaculated Mrs. Cottington ecstatically.

"But how on earth do the Mabels get their information?" added the chief inspector, with a humorous groan. "That's what beats me."

"Then I'll show you," whispered Mr. Cottington, as he

tiptoed across the room, and flung open the door with a sudden jerk.

The result was admirable.

"Mabel!" boomed Mr. Cottington. "Go back to your kitchen!"

An atmosphere of friendly confidence being thus induced, the Cottingtons vied with each other in giving their thrilling visitor all the information he wanted.

Put more briefly, this amounted to the interesting fact that No. 4 had, before its lease to the Danes, been vacant only a few weeks; six months ago it had been occupied, by an elderly spinster whose name was Miss Staples. Miss Staples had died last October, in consequence of which the house fell vacant.

This was not at all what Moresby had expected. He had taken it for granted that six months ago the house was either vacant, or occupied by a man who would prove to be the murderer. The character of Miss Staples, as the Cottingtons described it, seemed to shut out the remotest possibility of her being concerned in the crime in any way; she had been a gentle, feckless creature, incompetent in the most ordinary things of life and devoted to a fat pug and a fatter white Persian cat. How, then, had her house managed during her occupancy of it to acquire a very obviously murdered corpse under its cellar floor?

Here the Cottingtons were able to supply a valuable suggestion. Miss Staples had been away from her home for three weeks in August, on her annual holiday. It must have been during that period, Moresby considered, that her cellar had been put to this improper use.

He questioned them closely as to whether they had noticed

at any time during those three weeks any signs of improper occupancy of the house while its owner was absent, but they had noticed nothing. They had indeed been away themselves for the first fortnight in August.

Moresby obtained the exact dates of the Cottingtons' absence, and approximate ones for that of Miss Staples, and then, having asked the names of the occupiers of No. 6, took his leave with many expressions of genial gratitude.

The tenants of No. 6 were an elderly and retired insurance broker of the name of Williams, and his two elderly sisters. They also received the Scotland Yard man in a flutter of excitement, and the information received from their Mabel had first to be confirmed before questions could be asked.

These preliminaries settled, it appeared that they had known Miss Staples very well indeed, and while agreeing completely with the Cottingtons' estimate of her, were able to add a number of details to complete her picture in Moresby's mind. It became still more certain that Miss Staples must have remained in ignorance of what had happened in her cellar. Moreover when she came back from her holiday at the end of August she had said not a word to the Misses Williams as to her house having been entered in her absence; and both ladies gave it as their firm opinion that had Miss Staples noticed the slightest thing amiss she would certainly have spoken of it to them.

Had any of the three heard or noticed anything suspicious? Nothing; but then they had been on holiday themselves (Moresby was interested to hear) during the second and third weeks in August. Most curious, wasn't it, how everyone took their holidays in August, even people who had no real need to, like Miss Staples and themselves, although it really wasn't the best month for weather, and everyone knew that prices were much dearer; just habit; most curious. Most curious; it wasn't possible, was it, to fix the exact dates of Miss Staples's absence? Yes, indeed it was; Letty's diary; they all laughed at Letty for keeping a diary, but one never *knows*; diaries can sometimes be *most* useful; if it wasn't for Letty's diary, how could Mr. Moresby ever have found out such a thing as that?

Letty's diary was fetched, excitedly pored over, and finally divulged the information that Miss Staples had been away from the 6th of August to the 30th.

Neither of the two ladies had ever been in Miss Staples's cellar, of course? Why, indeed they had. Ever so many times. Was it kept empty? Oh, dear, no. It was full of the most *odd* sorts of lumber. Miss Staples kept *all* her old newspapers there for one thing: one never knew when old newspapers weren't going to come in handy, did one? No, never: what else did Miss Staples keep in her cellar? Oh, all sorts of bits of furniture, broken and *quite* useless; and packing-cases; and odd remnants of wall-paper; oh, and all the silly sorts of things one does keep in cellars. Was it chock-a-block, then? No, one certainly wouldn't call it that; there was plenty of room to move about. *Oh*, the chief inspector meant… Yes, indeed; it would have been quite easy to clear one corner, perhaps a whole half; and then if the things were put back again… How *horrible*! Yes, and just fancy: if Miss Staples hadn't died the—the murder might not have been discovered for *years*. Yes, Miss Staples had signed another seven years' lease only a few months earlier. Oh, she had, had she? Yes, she had. She always said she meant to die in that house, and oh, dear, oh, dear, died in it she had—and lucky not to be murdered in it too! Dear, dear, dear, what *was* the world coming to, Mr. Moresby? What was it indeed!

Now, what about Miss Staples's visitors? And her relations? Well, she didn't have many visitors; a few people in Lewisham, of course, and her neighbours in Burnt Oak Road; not more than a dozen all told. Could the Misses Williams make out a list, did they think, of the people Miss Staples knew? Oh, certainly they could; with pleasure; but surely Mr. Moresby didn't think…? Oh, no; just a matter of routine; one never knew; the most unlikely people were sometimes able to contribute helpful information. Relations? Well, there was a nephew; but such a *nice* young man; quite impossible that… his name and address? Well, his name was Staples too, but as for his address…wasn't he in the navy, Jane? Or was it the merchant service? Anyhow, Miss Staples called him "Jim," if that was any help. It was? How wonderful to think of oneself actually *helping* Scotland Yard!

Where was Miss Staples born? Oh, in Bath. Yes, very nice family. Miss Staples always spoke *very* well of her family. The Staples of Bath, yes. There had been a brother, but he was dead. Yes, he had been in business in Bristol. Something to do with advertising, but Miss Staples had never said very much about him; she had not thought advertising was really a very nice thing to be in; well, one does meet such *queer* people in advertising, doesn't one? Yes, perhaps one does: the nephew, then, was the son of the advertising brother? Yes, precisely. And he had a sister too; but she could not be a very nice girl, because she had never been to see her aunt—well, not for the last six years, since the Misses Williams had known her, at any rate. No, she had never spoken of any other relations, but no doubt there were cousins; there always are cousins, somehow, aren't there?

Moresby agreed that there always are cousins, somehow.

From No. 6, where he felt that he had been a good deal luckier than he had expected, he proceeded to the police station of the division. There he was informed that the records showed no complaint at the end of August or beginning of September, from Miss Staples of 4, Burnt Oak Road, that her house showed signs of having been tampered with during her absence; it was therefore quite certain that no such complaint had been made.

Moresby went back to No. 4.

The divisional inspector and his sergeant, their hands blue and their noses red but their devotion to duty unshaken, were working their way through the second of the four bedrooms. They eyed the chief inspector's warm presence with chilly gloom.

"Keep on looking," Moresby encouraged them. "You won't find anything, but keep on looking. Afford back?"

The divisional inspector explained that Sergeant Afford had reported back, and been sent off on the track of the house-agent. "Have you found out anything, Mr. Moresby?" he added.

"I've fixed the date of the murder," Moresby grinned, "if you call that anything. At least, within a week."

"You have, sir? When was it, then?"

"Second week of last August," said Moresby, and explained why. "And what's more," he added, "the murderer must have come in with a key. Now, I wonder how he got hold of that?"

CHAPTER II

THE ENQUIRY INTO THE DEATH OF THE YOUNG WOMAN found in the cellar at Burnt Oak Road proceeded on its routine course. The Press, of course, seized on it avidly. If, as Miss Rose Macaulay says, women are news, and by that presumably meaning live women, murdered young women are super-news. Young women, in the eyes of Fleet Street, are invariably romantic; and to be murdered in a suburban villa and buried under its cellar floor is obviously the quintessence of romance. Banner headlines flaunted their boldest type over double-column stories for just seven times as long as would have been the case if the victim had been an unnewsy young man. The Mabels of Burnt Oak Road had their lives' ambitions gratified.

Before he had gone home on the evening of the discovery, Moresby had telephoned through to the Bristol police for particulars of the son and daughter of advertising Mr. Staples, late of that city. The possession on the part either of murderer or victim of a key to 4, Burnt Oak Road, as seemed clearly evidenced by the lack of any signs of forcible entry, appeared to Moresby to point to one of the pair being connected in some way with Miss Staples herself, and he was hopeful that the murdered woman would prove to be the niece. At any rate, the first line of enquiry was plainly in that direction.

The next morning Moresby devoted entirely to the case. First of all Sergeant Afford was interviewed. He had seen the house-agent from whom the Danes had taken the house, at his home on the previous evening, but had been able to obtain no information of real value from him. On Miss Staples's death, her nephew, who was her sole heir (Afford thought there had been some trouble with the niece), had put the house in his hands for disposal of the remainder of his aunt's lease. The house had only been empty for three weeks. Then Mr. Dane had taken over the lease and, so the agent had gathered, got married on the strength of his acquisition. So far as the agent could say, Mr. Dane had had no motive in taking the house other than the possibility it gave him of immediate marriage. He had not called in connection with the board displayed outside No. 4; he had merely enquired, quite hopelessly, whether they had any house at all in a quiet road at not too high a rental.

Afford had been able to obtain information about this nephew. His name was James Carew Staples, and he was third officer on the *Duchess of Denver*, one of the Western Navigation Company's passenger boats plying between Liverpool and South America. He was about twenty-nine, and unmarried. Before coming to Scotland Yard that morning, Afford had ascertained that the *Duchess of Denver* was at that moment one day out from Buenos Aires.

Moresby at once wrote out a radiogram addressed to James

Staples, on board, asking him to wireless the present where-abouts of his sister and to call at Scotland Yard immediately on his return to England.

Afford was then despatched to Lewisham to make further enquiries in Burnt Oak Road and the houses whose gardens backed on to it, as to suspicious movements or strangers noticed during the summer, and particularly in the second week of August.

Moresby then sent for the inspector whose services were at his disposal, and set him to checking up the lists of missing women for the second half of the previous year. When it is realised that no fewer than six thousand women are reported as missing every year to Scotland Yard, it will be seen that this task was no light one; especially as anxious relatives, while hastening to report the missing one's absence, hardly ever bother to report her return, as, in nineteen cases out of twenty, return she does.

To help the inspector in his weeding-out, he was given a copy of the doctor's preliminary report, which had been put on Moresby's table late the previous evening. In view of the time the body had been in the ground, this was necessarily sketchy as regards her appearance. The doctor had however been able to give the following indications:

HEIGHT: Five feet five inches.
FIGURE: Medium slim, but well covered.
HAIR: Medium brown, but might have been darker during life.
FEET: Small? Size four shoes.
TEETH: All sound.

A closer examination had still revealed no natural distinguishing marks on the body, but what looked like the remains of a thin scar, some three or four inches long, had been found on the outside of the right thigh, about halfway down. It was impossible to say what colour the eyes had been, or the shape of the nose; nor was it possible to estimate the age within closer limits than twenty to thirty, and even these were elastic. The body had been in the ground certainly not less than three months, and probably not more than nine; six months was a likely guess.

This meagre information Moresby sent down for incorporation in the next day's *Police Gazette*, with a note on the circumstances in which the body was found, and a request for information regarding any woman to whom the description might apply and who had been missing for the period given.

Lastly, a detective-constable was given the pair of gloves which had been taken from the dead girl's hands, and sent off to a firm of glove manufacturers to learn what he could about them; and a second one despatched to make enquiries of every builder and builder's merchant in London as to a single bag of cement having been sold to a private customer during the months of June, July, or August last year. As he gave this last man his instructions Moresby thought of Roger Sheringham. It is by such arduous and painstaking and quite unspectacular methods that Scotland Yard gets its results; Mr. Sheringham, Moresby thought with a small grin, would be most scornful about them.

Having thus set the wheels of his machine in motion, the chief inspector rang through to Superintendent Green to ask if he might come along to the latter's room and discuss the case.

It was the superintendent's custom, before he voiced his own ideas about a case, to hear those of the officer in charge of it. He therefore began the conference with a grunted request to Moresby to sketch out the lines on which he proposed to conduct the investigation, and why.

Moresby explained the steps he had already taken, which met with a short nod not so much of approval as absence of disapproval, and then went on to give his views about the case in general.

"It seems to me, sir, that there are two ways of approach: was either the murderer or the girl connected with Miss Staples, or were they both complete strangers? In the first case, you see, we ought to be able to get a line through Miss Staples, in the second we can only get one through the girl's identity. I propose to work along both lines, of course."

The superintendent was understood to mutter to the effect that once the girl was identified the case would probably be as plain as a pikestaff.

"Yes," agreed the chief inspector, in a rather worried tone, "but to tell the truth, Mr. Green, I'm not too hopeful about identification. It's a long time, you see, and there's precious little for the relatives to swear to. We'll probably have her identified forty times over, if I know relatives."

"No wedding-ring."

"No rings at all. But that doesn't say there never were any. And it's impossible to say whether there were any marks of rings, or not; I looked particularly for that. No, I'm not relying too much on getting her identified through herself, so to speak; it's my belief that it'll turn out easier to get a line on the man, and identify her through him.

And that's why I propose to work the Miss Staples end for all it's worth."

"Unless it turns out to be the niece." The superintendent had already had Moresby's report, drawn up late on the previous evening, and was informed of everything that had been discovered up till then.

"Ah, yes, sir; and that's just what I'm hoping it will turn out to be," Moresby admitted. "That would make things nice and easy for us, that would."

"But apart from that, you think one of them was connected with Miss Staples?"

"I do; and there's two things that make me think so. How else did the murderer know that house was going to be empty, and the houses on each side of it too, in the second week in August? (I'm assuming that's when it was done.) How did he get in without leaving any traces—and you can bet the old lady didn't leave any windows open or the back door unlocked—if it wasn't with a key, and how did he get hold of a key, or the chance to get a key cut, if he didn't know her, and pretty well at that? Of course, both of those apply equally well to the girl; she could have passed 'em on."

"Something in that. Obviously premeditated, as I said yesterday. What about the cement? You think he had that there all ready?" Both officers were taking it for granted that the murderer was a man.

"It seems likely, doesn't it, sir? And a bag, to take her clothes away in. It wouldn't need to be a large one, the way girls' clothes are nowadays. We're dealing with a cunning one, all right; he had everything cut and dried beforehand. And what I mean is, he *must* have known some time ahead that he'd have that bit of the road to himself then, and how could he possibly, have known it if he hadn't got it (or she hadn't got it) from Miss Staples herself?" And Moresby, feeling that he had stated the argument as forcibly as was possible, permitted himself a mild beam.

"That's sound enough—*if* the murder was committed in that particular week. But you've not got the smallest evidence that it was."

"Well, no, Mr. Green, I haven't," the chief inspector confessed, a little dashed. "But it looks to me like a safe bet."

"We can't rely on safe bets," he was told severely. "We must have evidence. You know that. But there's no harm," added the superintendent more kindly, "in taking it as a working assumption, and seeing if you can get anything on it. Now, what about the girl? Putting the niece out of the question for the moment, have you got any ideas about her?"

"Well, no, sir; I can't say I have. Have you?"

The superintendent drew for a moment or two at his pipe before he answered.

"In this sort of case it usually turns out to be husband and unwanted wife. The Rainshill business. Remember? Deeming. Buried her, and two kids, under the hearth. But that's when they're the occupiers. I don't remember any other case where a house actually in the occupation of someone else, was made use of this way. That ought to give us something in itself, oughtn't it?" He puffed at his pipe again. Moresby waited in interested silence. The super, when he chose, could put two and two together as well as anyone.

"It shows a high level of intelligence, for one thing. It was safer than an empty house, you see, with all that junk in the cellar. And though it looks as if more nerve was wanted, it isn't really, if you've the sense to realise it. He had bad luck. It ought never to have been discovered at all. Yes, he's certainly of a higher type than the Rainshill man; and therefore probably, but not certainly, of a higher social class.

"You get that in the girl too, don't you? Size four shoes. And those gloves looked to me about six-and-a-half. Small hands and feet, sound teeth, well nourished. The gloves weren't cheap ones either, you noticed. Yes, I think we can call her a lady. Of the professional class at a guess, both of them. That should help you with those lists.

"Then what about their relations with each other? Intimate, obviously. Why does a man want to get rid of a woman—a young woman? Because she's become a nuisance to him. And that means almost invariably that she's standing in his way with another woman. She must have been under his influence. She accompanies him, you see, to someone else's house, and down they go to the cellar. I wonder what excuse he gave for that. They must have gone almost straight there too, because she still has her outdoor things on; hasn't even taken off her gloves."

"Unless he put them on her after she was dead, to mislead us in some way," Moresby ventured to put in. "I've wondered about that, because of the absence of rings. It isn't natural for a girl to wear no rings at all, is it? And if he took them off her, he must have had her glove off to do it. Well, why should he put the glove on again, instead of taking it away with the rest of her things?"

"May be something in that," agreed the superintendent. "It certainly looks as if he had some idea or other about those gloves. Well, you've got to find out what it was, that's all."

The telephone on the superintendent's desk tinkled, and he lifted the receiver. "Yes? Yes, put it through here. Bristol," he explained to Moresby. "You'd better take it."

Much of Bristol's information duplicated, and confirmed, that obtained by Sergeant Afford. With regard to the niece, Bristol was not helpful. She had left the town on her father's death five years ago, and the authorities knew no more about her. They were however enquiring among those of Mr. Staples's friends who might have kept in touch with her and hoped to have something further to report later in the day. In the meantime all they could say was that her age was thirty-one, and she had been unmarried when heard of last. Mrs. Staples died in 1907.

"Humph!" observed Superintendent Green, when this had been communicated to him. "Got to wait for the radio from her brother, then. Well, that's enough theorising. You'd better get on with it."

Moresby went back to his own room. There was little more he could do at the moment, and he occupied himself in drawing up an official paragraph for the evening papers, on much the same lines as that for the *Police Gazette*, giving the dead girl's description and asking for information. The papers could be trusted to embellish it with cajolery to their readers to recognise even from such sparse details somebody known to them; and though the inevitable result would be a flood of false identifications, each of which would have to be carefully enquired into, there was a good possibility that among them would be the correct one. In any case, it was the most hopeful line that offered at the moment. A helpful Press at their backs is one of Scotland Yard's greatest assets.

Just as Moresby was thinking of going out to lunch his telephone-bell rang. It was the police surgeon who, with a colleague, had been spending the morning in conducting the post-mortem on the body.

"Well, we're through, thank heaven," he told Moresby, "and I hope you don't find any more corpses in cellars for a long, long time. You'll get my report later. I'm just ringing you up now to give you one bit of information red-hot, in case it helps you. In fact so far as I can see it's the only thing we've found that's likely to be of the slightest help to you. She was going to have a child. About five months gone."

"Ah!" said Moresby, with great satisfaction. "Well, that gives us the motive at any rate. Thank you, Doctor."

CHAPTER III

THE RADIOGRAM FROM JAMES STAPLES REACHED
Moresby that afternoon. He gave his sister's address as a
girls' school in Berkshire, and Moresby took his inspector off
his lists in order to send him down to see her. It may be said
at once that the inspector found the younger Miss Staples
alive and extremely well at the school, where she worked as
personal secretary to the headmistress, that she was able to
prove that she had been abroad with two other mistresses
during the whole of the previous August, that she had scarcely
known her aunt, and that she was unable to throw any light
on the affair whatsoever. And that was the end of Moresby's
hopes concerning her.

He was not unduly cast down. Scotland Yard has to follow
up so many false trails before it hits the true one, that the latter
is cause for elation rather than the former for disappointment.

In this particular case, however, Moresby could not help
feeling that the number of false trails seemed even greater
than usual, and the number of pointers towards the true one

even less in evidence. Beyond the fact that she was about to have a child, the surgeon's report on the post-mortem added nothing at all to his knowledge of the dead girl. The cement clue petered out; after an enormous amount of work no mysterious single bag of cement could be traced, and every one of which there was a record was accounted for.

The gloves seemed to afford no help. The manufacturers of them were quickly found, but the pattern was a standard one; while not cheap they had not been expensive, and had been turned out in hundreds of pairs. It was impossible to follow any individual pair to its purchaser.

Nor was James Staples any more use. He called promptly at Scotland Yard as soon as he reached England, but though Moresby had a long interview with him nothing of the faintest interest came of it. He had only taken a bare look into the cellar after his aunt's death. As soon as he had gone through her papers he had sold the entire contents of the house to a firm of second-hand furniture merchants. He could suggest nothing at all. Moreover he had a quite unbreakable alibi for July, August, and September, not having set foot in England at all during those months.

More time was wasted in checking this alibi before the chief inspector was satisfied, and a little more still in interviewing the furniture firm, whose men had noticed nothing.

In the meantime other enquiries were quietly in progress.

An immense amount of labour went to the ferreting out of all Miss Staples's friends and acquaintances, all of whom were questioned as to their whereabouts during the last three weeks of August, and in some cases, beginning with Mr. Cottington (to that gentleman's indignation, had he ever known of it), these statements were very carefully checked; and though the result was that half a dozen people, mostly in Burnt Oak Road, *might* have committed the crime, there was nothing at all to show that any one of them had.

A laconic note was also sent down one day from the superintendent's room to the chief inspector's; "What did Miss Staples die of?" Moresby followed up the implication, looked up Miss Staples's death certificate, and interviewed the doctor who had signed it; but there was no doubt that Miss Staples had died naturally.

Three weeks running did the case come up at the weekly pow-wow, and on each occasion Moresby had to admit that no progress at all had been made, although three or four men had been working on it continuously.

At last the assistant commissioner sent for him.

Superintendent Green was in the room too, and both looked grave. Moresby, though he felt he had done all mortal man could do, was yet put on the defensive. As he sat down in the chair to which the assistant commissioner nodded, he felt uneasy; it is not enough for superintendents and assistant commissioners that their chief inspectors should do all mortal man can do, they expect more still.

The assistant commissioner had the dossier of the case before him, and he flicked over the pages absently as Moresby recounted the means by which he had tried to get to the bottom of it.

"And what do you think, Superintendent?" he asked, when the chief inspector had finished.

"I think, sir, that there's been too much concentration on the Miss Staples line of approach. Moresby's told us that his opinion still is that the thing was done by somebody who knew Miss Staples personally, because of the apparent use of a key to the house; but that isn't proved at all."

"Or he thinks that the girl might have been known to her," added the assistant commissioner.

"I did, sir," Moresby put in. "But we've checked up, so far as we could, every single woman between the ages of eighteen and forty whom Miss Staples seems to have known, and there's not one of them missing."

"You can't put the age limits closer than that?" asked the assistant commissioner, rather petulantly.

"All the doctor could say was that it was the body of an adult, and there were no signs of arthritis in the bones of the spine, as usually in the case of an elderly person. He guessed the age limits as twenty-two to thirty, but he warned me that might be a few years wrong at either end."

"Humph," said the assistant commissioner.

"*I* think, sir," pursued Superintendent Green, firmly bringing the discussion back from this irrelevance, "that *as* we can't say for certain that either the murderer or the girl was known to Miss Staples, and *as* all enquiries along that line have come to dead ends, we ought to concentrate on getting the girl identified. As I said to Moresby right at the beginning, once she's identified, the chances are a pound to a penny that our troubles are at an end."

"But he says he can't identify her. That's so, Moresby?"

"Yes, sir. Inspector Fox and Sergeant Afford have worked through not only the whole of last year's lists of missing women and girls, but the last six months of the year before that."

"You don't think they can have missed her?"

"I don't think so, sir. They've been very careful. Every single woman who's been found to be missing still has had her description compared with the dead girl's, and we've interviewed any number of the relations; and in each case there was some vital point of difference. I checked all their results myself. I'm satisfied that this girl was never reported as missing at all."

"And you got no help from the appeals through the Press?"

Moresby sighed as he thought of all the strenuous work to which those appeals had led, but all he said was: "None at all, sir."

There was a despairing little silence.

Superintendent Green broke it by saying, quite simply:

"That woman *must* be identified, Moresby."

Moresby said nothing. There was nothing to say.

But for all that the superintendent and the assistant commissioner said it. They said it at considerable length; but when Moresby left them half an hour later it had all amounted to nothing more than a repetition of Green's ultimatum: the woman *must* be identified.

It was an unhappy chief inspector who was allowed at last to retire to the refuge of his own room. That his position depended on a successful solution of the crime he knew was not the case; but that his prestige with his superiors did, had been made, only too plain. There had been too many unsolved murders during the last couple of years, had been the burden of the assistant commissioner's dirge; the papers had taken to printing a list of them whenever a new crime was announced, not with a comment but with comments very obviously omitted; this case had attracted even more of the public attention than usual; it *must* be solved.

That his superiors had been demanding the almost impossible from him, they had not hidden; but nevertheless they had demanded it.

His head on his knuckles, Moresby flogged his brains to find a way of identifying a totally unidentifiable corpse.

It was nearly an hour before an idea came to him. It was not a very promising idea, but at any rate it was an idea, and as such would show zeal if nothing else. He seized his telephone and put through a call to the surgeon who had conducted the post-mortem.

"Doctor," he said, "you remember that woman we found in the cellar in Lewisham?"

"Do I not!" replied the other, with feeling.

"You didn't by any chance X-ray the body, did you?"

"I did not. Why should I? You don't imagine," said the surgeon humorously, "that she'd been swallowing nails you could trace, or anything like that, do you? Because if so I can tell you at once that she hadn't."

"I only wanted to make sure you hadn't X-rayed her, sir," replied Moresby mildly.

He followed the call with one to the assistant commissioner, and put his request.

"An exhumation order?" repeated that gentleman, more than a little dubiously. "But what good do you think an X-ray photograph will do, Chief Inspector?"

"I don't know, sir," Moresby said with candour. "But you never know, do you? There might be a knitting-needle in her arm, or a bit of something in her foot for which she'd had treatment. It's clutching at a straw, I admit, but it can't do any harm and there doesn't seem to me much else than straws left to clutch at."

"Well, as you say, it can't do any harm, and I agree with you that we're rather reduced to straws. Anyhow, I'll put in for an order, but don't be surprised if the Home Secretary won't grant one, as we've no definite reason for wanting the X-ray."

The Home Secretary however did grant one; he was just as worried over the lists of unsolved murders as the assistant commissioner, and in any case, the woman not having been identified, there was no relation to make a fuss about exhumation. Besides, had Moresby but known it, he too realised that it showed zeal, and zeal was at any rate something to offer the public.

The corpse was disinterred, X-rayed, and photographed from all angles, and retained in the mortuary pending Moresby's pleasure before being returned to its unnamed grave.

Moresby talked over the results with the doctor, poring over the eerie photographs in an effort to pick out something which might conceivably serve his purpose.

"My dear Chief Inspector, there's nothing," he was assured. "I told you it would be a waste of time, and a waste of time of course it was. All we've learnt is that once she broke her leg, and what use you can make of that I'd be glad to hear."

Moresby jabbed a large forefinger at one of the photographs. "You mean this dark thing here?"

"I do. That dark thing is what is known as a plate; that is, a strip of metal used to hold the splintered ends of bone together if they don't unite by natural means. You screw it on to the bone. Remember I told you there were signs of a scar five or six inches long on the right thigh? That's where the incision was made."

"Very interesting, sir. Wonderful what you doctors can do nowadays. Quite a common thing, I suppose?"

"Oh, quite; you can hardly get a clue out of that. As a matter of fact, it isn't quite so common with the femur as with some of the other bones, but far too ordinary for you to be able to isolate any individual case. It might have been done at any time, you see."

"There wouldn't be anything to show how long ago? Or how old she was, even?"

"How old? No, not possibly; except that she was an adult. As to when it was done, I could probably tell, if I opened it up, whether it had been fractured within twelve months or so of death, from the extent and consistency of the callus; but once that's fully formed, it's out of the question even to make a guess."

"I see. So if she was forty years old, and it wasn't done within twelve months of death, it might have been done any time since she was eighteen?"

"It might. And though I wouldn't like to make a guess at how many fractured femurs are set with plates in the British Isles in the course of a year, I can tell you at once that there are a good many more than you could trace out with all the inspectors and sergeants in this place to help you, if you're to cover a period of only ten years."

"And we don't even know that it was done in the British Isles," mourned the chief inspector, and then stiffened as if a sudden idea had occurred to him.

The doctor's next words caused him to relax again.

"Oh, the plate would probably tell you that," he said carelessly. "They're usually stamped with the manufacturing firm's mark, or initials."

"They are, are they, sir?" Moresby said briskly. "Then that settles it. I'd like that plate, if you please, Doctor."

"Eh? But what on earth do you imagine you could do with it? The hospitals keep no record of what particular maker's plate was used in a case."

"But they do keep a record of whether a plate was used at all?"

"Oh, yes; they record that. But as I said just now, the amount of investigation would be impossible; and even if you could do it, the chances are thousands to one against your getting any result. Ten to fifteen years! Why, a large proportion of the patients would be dead and buried in that time; and I hardly suppose you're going to apply for exhumation orders for the lot of them."

"Nevertheless, I think I'll have that plate, sir," replied Moresby doggedly. "You never know."

"I do," the doctor retorted, with some annoyance. He had wanted never to see that body again.

Secretly, Moresby knew that the doctor must be right. On the other hand the plate was a definite, visible, tangible clue— the only one, apart from the useless gloves, that the case had offered, and as such he felt that he must have it. Though what he expected to do with it when he had got it, he would have had some difficulty in saying just then.

What he did do with it, twenty-four hours later, was to take it to the firm who had made it and, knowing that he was going to be laughed at but prepared to brave even that in the cause of duty, ask them what idea they could give him of its adventures since it was on their premises last.

He was laughed at.

Then the manager suddenly stopped laughing and began to examine the plate more closely.

"Well," he said at last, "you're in luck, Chief Inspector. In nine hundred and ninety-nine cases out of a thousand it would be simply impossible to give you an answer, beyond a list of the hospitals that we've supplied with that type of plate for the last twenty years. But in this case, just as it happens..."

"Yes?" Moresby prompted eagerly.

"Well, the odds aren't quite so much against you."

The manager, a dry little man with a Scotch accent, settled his spectacles on his nose with much deliberation, and scrutinised the plate again in an affectionate way.

"How does that come about?" Moresby prompted again.

"Why, in this way. About five or six years ago, so far as I remember—or maybe only four: anyhow I can find that out from the books. A few years ago we made a batch of plates out of a new alloy that we hadn't used before. I can't rightly remember what the components were, and no doubt the question won't interest you; but the thing is that we didn't make very many of them. It was in the nature of an experiment, you see. And it wasn't very successful. We got reports that the plates weren't sufficiently malleable. So we didn't use that alloy any more."

"And this is one of them?"

"On each of them," pursued the manager, who was a man not to be hurried, "we put a special sign after our initials, seeing that it was by way of an experiment, you understand. I recognise that mark here."

"And how many did you make of them?"

"One hundred. One hundred exactly, no more and no less. I remember perfectly."

"This is going to help me a lot," said Moresby with enthusiasm. "I was wondering whether I was ever going to have the bit of luck with this case that we nearly always do get in the ones we're successful with. One per cent luck and ninety-nine per cent hard work, Mr. Ferguson, that's what detecting is; and neither of them a bit of use without the other. Now I take it that as this was an experiment of yours, the hospitals will for once have kept a record of the cases in which these plates were used?"

Mr. Ferguson shook his head and looked less elated. "No, they won't have done that. And for this reason: we didn't tell them it was an experiment. It doesn't concern them what alloy is used so long as the plate is satisfactory; and with our reputation, any plate we supply is bound to be that. These just weren't perfection. So I don't see that this is going to help you much after all."

"Oh, yes, it is, sir," replied Moresby benignly. "You just look up in your books the date when you sent the first of these out, and the date of the last, and I think I can tell you that it's going to help me very considerably."

CHAPTER IV

THE DATES WHICH MORESBY TRIUMPHANTLY CARRIED away with him were the 27th April, 1927, and the 14th July of the same year. Before he left he asked the little manager how long a hospital might be expected to keep a plate in stock, and was told that it was impossible to say; once a plate was put into the permanent stock it might stay there indefinitely.

Nevertheless, Moresby was triumphant. His possible twenty years had been reduced to far more manageable dimensions. The date of the discovery of the body was the 22nd of February, 1931. The doctor had now guaranteed that the body had been in the ground for not less than four months. When removing the plate he had examined the callus and was able to affirm that the fracture was not less than a year old. That took one back sixteen months, say to the end of August, 1929. Moresby had not the least idea how many fractured femurs had been set with plates in Great Britain between the 27th April, 1927, and the 31st August, 1929, but he was going to make it his business to find out.

As soon as he got back to Scotland Yard he drafted out an urgent letter of which a copy was sent to every hospital and nursing-home in the British Isles. There was still the possibility that the operation had not been performed in the British Isles at all and that the unknown woman was a foreigner, since the little manager had stated that his firm did quite a considerable export business; but Moresby considered Great Britain enough for a beginning. Also that sixth sense of the experienced detective told him that he was firmly on the trail of the girl's identity at last.

As the replies to his letter began to come in, there followed for Moresby and the officers working under him a period of that unremitting, dogged routine labour of which the public hears nothing and to which no reference is ever made at the trial, but which to the Scotland Yard man constitutes nine-tenths of his normal work. It was found that during the period in question, six hundred and forty-one women had had fractured right femurs set with plates. Of these it was possible to eliminate, under age or other headings, two hundred and nineteen. Each single one of the remaining four hundred and twenty-two had to be traced from hospital to home, to lodging, or to present abode of whatever description, from place to place, often with the greatest difficulty and necessitating a dozen interviews to establish a single move, until finally run to earth and proved to be alive, or run to earth and proved to be legally and innocently dead.

Whenever possible, and of course there was a fairly large proportion of simple cases, the work was entrusted to the local detective forces of the districts and counties concerned; but even so the amount of it which fell directly on Moresby's shoulders was prodigious. For nearly three months he was constantly on the move, travelling up and down the country in search personally of the most elusive cases (and it was astonishing how many of them had removed themselves so far and so frequently in less than four years), now and then taking a swoop right across England to the rescue of the less experienced Inspector Fox and Sergeant Afford, who were working with him, when either found himself baffled, keeping in continual touch with Scotland Yard, and altogether behaving with an energy and agility not in the least to be looked for in a middle-aged man of his appearance and bulk.

Gradually references to the case in the Press grew shorter and fewer, and finally appeared no more; gradually it slipped out of the untenacious memory of the public. And while those who did still remember it added it automatically to London's formidable list of unsolved mysteries, the beaver-like work went on and on until one afternoon in late June, Chief Inspector Moresby, sitting in his room in Scotland Yard, was able to cross off his list four hundred and twenty-one names, so that only one was left.

"…last heard of in Allingford," wrote the chief inspector in his report, "where she—" He stopped writing and began to chew the end of his pen. What particular connection with Allingford was hiding somewhere in his mind?

Allingford, of course, is on the borders of the metropolitan police district, a good twelve miles from Charing Cross. It is not a suburb of London, for there is open country between the two. Moresby was not sure that he had ever been in the place at all before this enquiry took him there. Why then did it now occur to him all of a sudden that there was some particular significance in the girl having been traced to Allingford—yes, and to that particular school in Allingford, too?

He remembered. Mr. Sheringham had mentioned casually last summer that he had been deputising, more for a joke than anything for he had no need to do anything of the sort, for a master who had gone sick, at his old preparatory school of Roland House, in Allingford. Moresby had only listened perfunctorily, as he did to most of Mr. Sheringham's chatter (that is, when Mr. Sheringham was not chattering very much to the point about a case in which Moresby was interested), but now the remark took on a very great importance. Last summer...and at Roland House too...

Moresby reached for his telephone and gave Mr. Sheringham's number.

Mr. Sheringham was out.

Moresby, who was a man of very great patience, took up his pen again and went on with his report.

After he had had his dinner that evening he tried again, this time with better luck. Mr. Sheringham was in, and would be delighted to receive Moresby.

"I got a new cask in three days ago," he said with enthusiasm. "It's the real stuff—Berkshire XXXXX, and better beer there never was. It should have settled by now. We'll broach it together."

"I'll be along in fifteen minutes, Mr. Sheringham," said Moresby, with scarcely less enthusiasm.

A bus took him to the Albany, and with a nod to the porter he made his way to Roger Sheringham's rooms.

Roger was looking through a batch of American press-cuttings on his last book when Moresby arrived, and appeared to be considerably entertained by them. For a few minutes the author in him ousted the detective, while he read out to the chief inspector some of the choicer extracts.

"Listen, Moresby. The *Outlook and Independent*: 'We were puzzled by the use in conversation of the phrase "I'll buy it" until it occurred to us that it was probably an English author's rendering of the American slang "I'll bite."' Rather pleasant, that. It doesn't occur to the man that it might be an English author's rendering of English slang, you see; it just simply doesn't occur to him.

"The *Chicago News* is terribly severe with me. It bumps me off in the most approved fashion. 'An ingenious plot, woefully overstuffed with ponderous attempts at humour by a thoroughly unhumorous author.' No taking the *Chicago News* for a joy-ride, you see. Personally, I prefer the *New York Herald-Tribune* which says, only ten days after I've been bumped off in Chicago: 'His mischievous manner is a godsend for the less owlish addicts.' Can it be, Moresby, do you think," asked Roger with awe, "that the *Chicago News* is an owlish addict?"

Roger was so overcome with the solemnity of this thought that the cask of XXXXX had to be broached, and the health of the *Chicago News* reverently drunk, before Moresby could get down to his own business.

"You remember, Mr. Sheringham, telling me last summer that you were going down to Allingford to take the place of a master who was ill at a school called Roland House. Did you ever go?"

Roger looked at him suspiciously. Whenever Moresby spoke in that extremely casual tone it meant that his subject was an important one. "I did, yes. Why?"

"When were you there?"

"For a fortnight in the middle of July. Why?"

"Would that be the end of the term?"

"Not quite. The other man came back for the examination week. I'd had enough of it by then and left. Why?"

"What made you go there at all, Mr. Sheringham?"

"The man whose place I took is a friend of mine. When I heard he was ill I offered to take his job on for a fortnight or so, as a change of occupation. The truth was that I'd been contemplating a novel with the setting of an English preparatory school and wanted to collect a little local colour, but that's between ourselves. Why?"

Moresby took a long pull at his tankard and then wiped his heavy moustache with deliberation. "You remember that girl who was found under a cellar floor in a house in Lewisham about four months ago?"

"Yes. You people haven't been able to discover who she was, let alone who shot her."

"Well, we know now who she was; and I think it will interest you to hear that she came from Roland House."

Roger stared. "Good heavens, Moresby—somebody I knew?"

"I presume so, sir, if you were there for a fortnight."

"What was her name?"

The chief inspector shook his head. "That, if you don't mind, we're keeping quiet for the moment, Mr. Sheringham."

"Even from me?"

"Even from you, sir."

Roger seemed too upset even to protest.

Moresby looked at him curiously. He had not expected Mr. Sheringham to take his news so hardly.

"A funny sort of coincidence," he said lamely.

"Coincidence! That's just what I'm afraid it isn't, Moresby? I've got a horrible feeling that in a way I'm responsible for that girl's death."

"How do you make that out, Mr. Sheringham?" asked Moresby, startled himself.

"Why, I remember distinctly one evening at dinner... They'd been egging me on to talk about murder—and I don't need much egging on to talk, as you may have noticed," said Roger, with a gloomy smile. "I can remember quite well that I talked about the extraordinary foolishness of the average murderer who gets caught. I told them that for an ordinarily intelligent man murder should be a picnic, and the simplest precautions are enough to insure against detection. I gave them, in fact, a sort of lecture on murder, not as a fine art but as a practical means of getting rid of an unwanted person. I talked a lot of damned rot, of course, but then I always do. I never dreamed that any one of them could be taking me seriously: but it looks very much as if one of them did."

"Who was present on the occasion?" asked Moresby officially.

"Oh, everyone. The whole staff. We always dined together. I say, Moresby, it wasn't that nice Mrs. Harrison, was it?"

Moresby shook his head. "I won't tell you just yet, if you don't mind. I've a reason. That's what I've come to see you about. I want you to give me your unbiased impressions of the people there, and tell me if you noticed anything going on under the surface at all."

"Under the surface!" Roger echoed, with a little laugh. "It's plain you've never been on the staff of a preparatory school towards the end of term, Moresby. There's nothing going on except under the surface. I never saw so many undercurrents among a small body of people in my life. All so petty, and all of them taking it so seriously."

"That's very interesting. Then—"

"Look here," Roger interrupted, "I've got it. You remember I told you I went down there to collect copy for a novel. Well, I collected it; any amount of it. And I began the novel. I got bored with it after I'd done a few chapters and put it aside, but I've still got the manuscript. I'll lend it you. That will tell you in far more detail than I could, my impressions of Roland House and what was going on there."

"You mean, you used the real people there for your book?"

"Well, of course. One always does that, in spite of the law of libel and the funny little notices some people put in the front of their books to say that all the characters in this story are imaginary. Imaginary my hat! Nobody could imagine a character and make it live. No, all the characters in my manuscript are transcribed as literally and as truthfully as I could manage it from Roland House, and if I give you a key to the changed names you'll know as much about the staff there as if you'd stayed among them for a fortnight. How's that?"

"That seems the very thing, Mr. Sheringham. That ought to help me quite a lot."

"You haven't settled on the murderer then?"

"No. We've made some enquiries there of course, but I'll confess to you that for all we know at the moment, it might have been any one of them. The motive's plain enough, but not the person who was going to benefit by it."

"That's just the sort of thing you ought to be able to get

from my manuscript," said Roger enthusiastically. "I ought to explain that I set the time forward a few days from my own observations, in order to allow the various pots which were only simmering then to come to the boil. And you must make allowances. I can't guarantee the truth of the details, but I'd stake my reputation as a prophet (if I had one) that the broad lines are right. There isn't a development in it which I didn't see in preparation; and you might say that there isn't an action for which I haven't definite evidence. It isn't difficult, you know, to forecast people's major actions when one has studied their minor ones. The mind never alters its sweep."

"Is that so?" said Moresby politely.

Roger was diving into the drawers of his desk. "Here it is. I've got a copy. You can keep that if you like. And now tell me which the woman is."

"Well, I don't see why I shouldn't now, Mr. Sheringham. You'll keep it to yourself, I know. In strict confidence, she was—No!" Moresby grinned suddenly. "I won't tell you after all."

"I can always ring up Roland House and find out who's not there now," Roger retorted, with a touch of petulance.

"Yes, you can do that, sir, of course. But what I was going to say was: I won't tell you now, I'll leave it to you to find out. You read through your copy of this, and if it's like you say, you ought to be able to pick out which girl it was who got murdered, oughtn't you?"

"Spot the victim, eh? Well, I won't guarantee it; for the reason that I can't promise to have seen everything that was going on under the surface. But it's a good idea, Moresby. I'll certainly try it."

PART II

Roger Sheringham's Manuscript[*]

CHAPTER V

I

TWENTY-FIVE YEARS AGO THE HAMLET OF ALLINGFORD had a population of about twenty-five persons, not including the fifty or so part-time residents of Roland House. Secure in its eleven miles of distance from Piccadilly Circus, and the fact that the London and North Western Railway missed it by nearly a league, it was able to think of London as something almost as remote as the mysterious and reputed inferno called Birmingham, which lay at the other end of the nearest main road. Twenty-five years ago a journey to London was an Adventure, not to be undertaken lightly or without due preparation.

To-day, contrary to the experience of most hamlets within eleven miles of Piccadilly Circus, Allingford is still little more than a large village. Its population does not exceed a mere and scattered six hundred. The London, Midland and Scottish Railway still lies nearly a league away, and even the voracious Overground has not stretched out a tentacle quite in its direction.

In the single street the same little three shops still flourish as flourished when King Edward came to the throne, and doubtless Queen Victoria before him; only one of the multiple stores has opened a branch there. Allingford, in short, is a deplorable exception to that spirit of progress which has made our England what she now is. There is, as a fact, no wine merchant's in Allingford; but if there were it is only too possible that he would sell you a half-bottle of whisky (that is, if you were depraved enough to wish to buy a half-bottle instead of a whole one) and never realise what a menace to modern society he was.

Allingford's regrettable condition is due of course to the fact that the road from London to Birmingham passes a mile away from its cottages and not through the midst of them. Only a mile away the stream of progress roars backwards and forwards; beaming men of business dart in portly cars on their respective ways, stockbrokers whiz along in the mistakes of other people about margins, chorus girls flit from Birmingham to London to display their legs or from London to Birmingham to conceal them. Allingford, a mere mile away, knows them not and, most lamentably, cares less.

It is not surprising therefore that amid such stagnation Roland House should be to the present generation of its inmates precisely what it was to their fathers before them. A new dormitory over the gymnasium, a tiled changing-room instead of a distempered one, a couple more acres of playing-fields snatched from the villa-hungry builder: these were almost the only changes in the last twenty-five years.

And, of course, the staff.

Twenty-five years ago Mr. Hamilton Harrison, M.A. (Oxon.), had been just Ham Harrison, the most junior of all junior masters, very green from the University; now he owns the place, and has done for the last six years. It is possible no doubt to save money, even on the salary of a junior master at a preparatory school, for there is no limit to what a determined man can do; but Mr. Hamilton Harrison had not had to be so determined as all that. It is indeed very doubtful whether he could have been. An easier course had been thrust upon him. The daughter of the then headmaster, a young woman with determination for two and to spare, had fixed her maidenly affections upon the gentle junior master and, almost before he knew what was happening to him, married him out of hand. She had lived long enough after that to inherit the school for him, presenting him in the meantime with one child, a daughter, and had then very firmly died.

Amy Harrison, now twenty-two years old, had taken after her mother. The school had thus been held together, as it were, under Mr. Harrison's nose. People spoke of Amy as a wonderful help to her father. Mr. Harrison agreed with them, as he agreed with most people. Privately he considered Amy a ghastly nuisance. She was always trying to make him do things he did not want to do, or urging action on him when Mr. Harrison very well knew that inertia would be more effective, besides less trouble.

She was doing just that thing now. In one hand she held a pair of young male pants, which she brandished at her parent like a banner while she spoke to him with force.

"Father, I *insist* on your looking at them properly."

"Take them away, Amy," returned Mr. Harrison peevishly. "Really, my study is no place for this kind of thing. Take them away."

"Full of holes. *Full* of them. Luckily I was in the room when Weston brought them in; otherwise of course I should never have heard about them. It's only a week to the end of term; it would have been a nice thing if he'd gone home with them like that, wouldn't it? What do you think his parents would say? Of course, I've ordered a general inspection of all underclothes; luckily there's still time; but if all of them are in that state, or even half..." Amy's voice trailed into indignant silence.

"Well, don't bother me with them. You know perfectly well how busy I always am at the end of term. Take them to Phyllis."

"Phyllis!"

Amy uttered a short, scornful laugh, but to Mr. Harrison's relief added nothing to it. Amy did not approve of her young step-mother; nor did she trouble to hide the fact, either from Phyllis Harrison herself or from her father.

She dropped now on to the arm of a chair and gazed at Mr. Harrison firmly. "I haven't come to bother you just with Weston's pants, father; you should know me better than that. It's what Weston's pants stand for."

"Well?" Mr. Harrison positively barked out the word, to cover his attempts to avoid his daughter's look, which always made him feel guilty of some unknown but particularly heinous enormity, just as her mother's had before her. "Well? Be quick, please, Amy. I'm really exceedingly busy. What do Weston's pants stand for?" He rustled some of the papers on his desk.

"This," Amy replied briskly. "Miss Jevons Must Go!"

Mr. Harrison, who all the time had known only too well what Weston's pants must stand for, coughed irritably. "Really, Amy, I can't see—"

"Miss Jevons Must Go!" Amy repeated inexorably.

Mr. Harrison began feebly to lose his temper. It was intolerable that Amy should come delivering ultimatums like this, trying practically to browbeat him in his own study. Was he never to have any peace? Everything seemed to conspire to harass him at the end of term, just when he was so extremely busy—masters with complaints against other masters, mistresses with complaints about servants, Amy with complaints about everyone. And now this bother over Miss Jevons, who was about the only person in the house who never complained about anything.

"Nonsense!" exploded Mr. Harrison. "I won't—"

"She was an experiment," Amy continued, just as if he had never exploded at all. "An experiment that hasn't answered. I shan't have a lady for a matron again; it doesn't do."

"*You* won't have..."

"Besides, she's far too young."

"Twenty-eight!"

"According to her own account."

"I see no reason to doubt it. She's an extremely pleasant girl, and the boys are very fond of her." Mr. Harrison was still spluttering but there would be no more explosions.

"She's inefficient," Amy summed up, tightening her rather thin lips, "and we simply cannot afford to have an inefficient matron." She rose. "Father, you know as well as I do that she must go. You must give her notice this week, the sooner the better, and I'll advertise for another." As if there was no more to be said, she walked out of the room with the offending pants.

Mr. Harrison gazed after the short but erect figure of his daughter. His momentary anger had evaporated, as usual, into a rebellious exasperation. He was not at all sure that he was going to do this time what Amy wanted; not at all sure. He liked Miss Jevons; the boys liked her; everyone liked her except Amy, who only liked efficient people; and undoubtedly Miss Jevons did her best.

For once Amy had overstepped herself. It was absurd, the way she took his consent for granted—her own father. Amy was really getting too officious altogether. Did she know what the boys called her? Mr. Harrison thought not. Certainly no one in the place would have dared to tell her. But if not, she was the only one who didn't. "Goggle-eyes!" It would do her good if someone did tell her. With all a parent's proverbial astigmatism Mr. Harrison could not attribute any beauty, or even prettiness to his daughter, with her thin lips, her long, thin, rather bluish nose, her sandy-coloured hair, and those rather conspicuous pale-blue eyes which had earned her her nickname. "Goggle-eyes!" It really was rather good. Mr. Harrison was unfeeling enough to chuckle guiltily.

His amusement was cut short by a knock at his door.

It was Miss Jevons, in tears.

"Oh, Mr. Harrison, please forgive me bothering you when I know you're so busy, but…but…"

"Well?" frowned Mr. Harrison, nervousness making his voice harsher than he had intended. Mr. Harrison detested giving people notice.

"I—I felt I must know if it's true. Miss Harrison said…"

"Miss Harrison had no authority to say anything," returned Miss Harrison's father, pulling in annoyance at his straggling grey beard. This was really too much of Amy. Whose school was it, anyhow?

"Sh-she said—you were going to give me notice," faltered Miss Jevons.

"Miss Harrison had no authority to say *anything*," repeated Mr. Harrison firmly. "In any case," he added, as much to his own surprise as to that of Miss Jevons, "that is quite untrue. I had no such intention."

"Oh, Mr. Harrison!"

Gratitude swam in Miss Jevons's hazel eyes. She was a tall girl, with a neat figure which her plain dress of pale-green linen made neater still; and she would have been pretty but for a mouth too large and a nose which even the most determined of magazine-writers could not have called "tip-tilted" instead of "snub." In Miss Harrison's opinion she wore her skirts a good deal too short; Mr. Harrison did not share his daughter's opinion; Miss Jevons had extremely well-shaped legs.

She dabbed at her eyes now with a most unmatronlike wisp of handkerchief.

"There, there," said Mr. Harrison benevolently.

"It was a shock," gulped Miss Jevons. "I've tried very hard. I thought I'd been... My mother, you know... We've only got what I earn."

"Of course, of course. It was unpardonable of Amy. Quite unpardonable."

Mr. Harrison rose from his desk, swinging his glasses on their thin black cord. He felt a different man now. Why could he not have had a daughter like this graceful, charming girl, to whom one really could be a father?

He laid his hands paternally on the charming girl's still quivering shoulders. "Just keep a closer eye on the boys' garments, my dear. They're young ruffians, you know. Just keep a closer eye on that sort of thing."

"Oh, I will, Mr. Harrison—I will."

"I'm sure you will, my dear." Mr. Harrison bent his head and kissed Miss Jevons, paternally but most unprofessionally, on the forehead.

Equally unprofessionally, but not at all filially, Miss Jevons threw her arms round his neck, gave him a swift but most efficient hug, kissed him warmly on the cheek, and ran out of the room. Once again Mr. Harrison found himself staring at a closed door; but this time with a very different expression on his face.

The expression gradually faded, to be replaced by a worried frown. Mr. Harrison's awkward length drooped once more in the chair before his desk.

The thought of Amy was seldom out of the mind of any inhabitant of Roland House for long.

II

The day was a hot one, towards the end of July.

In the masters' sitting-room the windows were wide open on to the big lawn at the back of the house. With pipes in their mouths and newspapers in their hands three men sprawled at ease. The time was that blessed half-hour after the midday meal before cricket begins, when only one master is on duty and the others get their first chance since breakfast to be human beings. A richly contented silence, broken only by the rustling of the newspapers and the bubblings of Mr. Parker's pipe, which could never be induced to behave quite as other men's pipes, filled the room.

For ten minutes there was no action, but for Mr. Duff's exchange of the *Daily Mail* for the *Morning Post*, and Mr. Rice's discarding of the *Daily Mirror* in favour of the *Daily Sketch*. Mr. Parker never read anything but *The Times*.

It was Mr. Rice who opened a topic of conversation.

This was not uncommon, in the masters' sitting-room. With a laboured courtesy, from which condescension was excluded obviously only with care and difficulty, Mr. Rice would address a remark to the company at large, as if bent on showing that to him at any rate there was no gap between his colleagues and himself, however conscious of such a thing they might be; for the present at any rate they were all on the same plane. For Mr. Rice, twenty-four years old and only two of them down from Cambridge, with a blue for cricket and a half-blue for swimming, had made no secret of the fact that the couple of years he was putting in at Roland House were makeshift ones only, while he awaited the vacancy which had been promised him at his own important public school.

"Yorkshire all out for under the century, I see," observed Mr. Rice kindly to the masters' sitting-room. "Pretty bad show."

Mr. Parker, who did not like Mr. Rice, lurked behind *The Times* and said nothing.

Mr. Duff poked his small head round the edge of the *Morning Post*, looking, as he often did, exactly like a tortoise in pince-nez, and smiled. "Really?" he said brightly. Then, as if realising that the failure of Yorkshire was no occasion for brightness, was indeed a pretty bad show, he switched his smile into a frown. "*Really?*" he said.

"Fact," Mr. Rice assured him.

Mr. Duff made a small sound, which might have been expressive of scorn, disappointment, disgust, chagrin, or indeed anything that suited Mr. Rice's convenience, and after blinking rapidly for a moment, withdrew his head again into the shell of the *Morning Post*.

"Looked as if they might develop into quite a decent batting side at the beginning of the season," added Mr. Rice, and out shot Mr. Duff's small, rather bald head again to nod vigorous confirmation of this late possibility. The fact that Mr. Duff had not so much as glanced at the cricket page in any newspaper for the last fifteen years, and that Mr. Rice was quite well aware of this deficiency, detracted in no way from the amenity of the exchange.

Mr. Parker, like Brer Rabbit, continued to lurk and say nothing. Unlike Brer Rabbit he emitted a vigorous upward blow through his rather bushy grey moustache.

This was a not uncommon phenomenon on the part of Mr. Parker. On this occasion, however, the blow was more vigorous than usual, and Mr. Duff at once and characteristically interpreted it, and this time quite correctly, as a wordless comment upon himself. His thin, sallow face flushed slightly as it darted back once more into its shell. If Mr. Duff had been capable of disliking anyone, he would have disliked Mr. Parker.

Mr. Rice tossed the *Daily Sketch* with a careless gesture into a corner of the room, as if to intimate that he was now ready to put aside the weightier things of existence and devote himself to brightening the drab lives of those about him.

"What was the row this morning between Harrison and Leila, eh?"

Whereas his colleagues invariably spoke of "Miss Jevons," the matron, "Miss Waterhouse," the governess, "Miss Harrison" and "Mrs. Harrison," it was Mr. Rice's more genial habit to refer to them respectively as "Leila," "Mary," "Amy," and "Phyllis."

At Mr. Rice's question Mr. Duff discarded his shell altogether. The *Morning Post* dropped across his knees. He looked vaguely apprehensive.

"What row?"

"I hear the old man had her on the carpet."

"Indeed?"

"She was weeping when she came out."

Mr. Duff's expression tautened. "I haven't heard anything about it."

"No?" Mr. Rice was now plainly bored with the subject. He had made old Duff sit up, and that was all he wanted. He took manly pity on his victim. "Cheer up, Duff. I don't suppose he sacked her, or it would have been all round the place by now."

"Yes." Mr. Duff looked relieved. "Yes; that's true, of course."

Mr. Parker blew through his moustache.

Mr. Rice yawned.

Mr. Duff, the *Morning Post* still on his knees, gazed thoughtfully through his rimless pince-nez at the garden outside.

Mr. Rice looked at *The Times*, a shield between Mr. Parker and such contacts as Mr. Parker did not welcome. Any kind of shield Mr. Rice looked on as a challenge.

He took a mild tilt at this one.

"Coming down to the field this afternoon, Duff?" he enquired, with perhaps rather more loudness than was quite necessary.

"This afternoon?" Mr. Duff repeated vaguely.

"Final of the cricket league."

Mr. Parker blew through his moustache.

Since coming to Roland House Mr. Rice, by virtue of his blue and a half, had of course taken the games in hand. He had dealt with them drastically. In cricket, for instance, he had revolutionised the batting style, briefly dismissing the strained attitudes hitherto cultivated and the worship of the straight bat, as old-fashioned tosh. Mr. Parker, who had reigned unquestioned in this kingdom for the last twenty years, looked on from the boundary in pain and distress, blowing contemptuously through his moustache. To Mr. Parker a straight bat was a holy thing, on a par with the House of Lords, the Athenaeum Club, *The Times*, and all those noble institutions for which Mr. Parker considered England stood.

It was therefore doubly distressing to Mr. Parker that the bats of Roland House should not only be no longer straight, but should have crookedly scored this season more runs than ever in history before. For the first time on record not a single school cricket match had been lost. Mr. Parker had continued to blow defiance through his moustache on the boundary, but more and more forcedly as the season progressed. Mr. Parker was not a blue.

Another innovation of Mr. Rice's had been the cricket league. The sixty odd boys had been divided into four teams, the Reds, the Blues, the Greens, and the Yellows, a team and a spare man apiece, and the remainder under the name of Reserves to encourage their players from the boundary. Mr. Parker had gone about muttering darkly of professionalism, but the scheme had been a success. In justice to himself, however, Mr. Parker continued to blow through his moustache whenever these evidences of the modern professional spirit in games were mentioned before him.

"Oh!" Mr. Duff now said guiltily. "Oh, yes; yes, of course. Yes, I must see that undoubtedly. The final, yes. That is, if I can get the Fourth's Latin grammar paper corrected in time." The day was a Monday, and the end-of-term examinations had begun that morning. It was Mr. Duff's terminal ambition to keep abreast of the papers for which he was responsible by getting each one corrected on the day it was done; an ambition which in fifteen odd years of schoolmastering had never once yet been fulfilled.

The conversation again lapsed.

Mr. Parker's shield remained undislodged.

Young Mr. Rice lifted his large body out of the chair and stretched it greatly. "Ah, well," he observed. "Must get along and change, I suppose. Promised I'd give Phyllis a spot of coaching on her backhand before the match. Bit of a nuisance sometimes, women, eh, Duff? Or don't they worry you?"

Mr. Duff smiled nervously.

Mr. Rice lumbered out of the room, his hands in his pockets and an expanse of grey-flannelled stern very much in evidence.

Mr. Parker lowered his shield at last.

"Insufferable young jackanapes," growled Mr. Parker, and blew so vigorously that it was a wonder his moustache remained on his lip at all.

III

In the matron's room three very excited young women were drinking tea. Reading from left to right, as the illustrated papers say, these were Miss Jevons, Miss Waterhouse, and Miss Crimp. Miss Waterhouse combined the duties of governess to the infants' class and secretary to the headmaster (which meant, more often, secretary to the headmaster's daughter); Miss Crimp taught music and dancing. Alone among the staff of Roland House (except for the Rev. Michael Stanford, who came on Monday mornings to take the sixth form in catechism and the scriptures) Elsa Crimp did not live on the premises. She was the daughter of a local artist, of some considerable reputation, and, like Mr. Rice, she let it be known that her presence at Roland House was in the nature of a kindness to that institution. At normal times Miss Crimp took pupils after lunch; she had forgotten that this was examination week and music lessons were in abeyance, and so found that she had arrived at Roland House that afternoon to no purpose. Naturally, therefore, she had wandered up to Miss Jevons's room—to learn that she had not arrived to no purpose after all.

Leila Jevons was one of those women who can never keep a good thing to themselves. Whatever entered the field of Miss Jevons's experience trickled out again through her mouth. She had just finished telling her two enthralled listeners, for the third time, the story of Mr. Harrison's Astounding Behaviour. It was a good story, and it got better with each repetition.

"My dear, how terrible for you," said Mary Waterhouse, with big eyes.

"I had to let him, you see," explained Miss Jevons, with pleased masochism, "or I'd probably have got the push after all. I bet Amy had done her best to make him give it me, curse her. And all over a wretched pair of pants, my dear."

"Well, I should never have thought Mr. Harrison was *that* sort," said Miss Waterhouse.

"Hasn't he ever tried anything like that on with you?"

"I should hope not," exclaimed Miss Waterhouse virtuously. "He knows I wouldn't let a married man mess *me* about." Miss Waterhouse, as everyone knew, was a stickler for duty. Her favourite expression was, "One does one's job." She was quite pretty enough to have been nothing of the sort.

"Nonsense!" observed Miss Crimp robustly. "You know perfectly well you would, Mary, if you thought he was really interested. You're sexually starved, just as Leila is. You're both ready to fall into the arms of the first man who opens them, married or not." As the daughter of an artist Miss Crimp cultivated a healthy, if somewhat self-conscious, unconventionality. Her favourite expression was "sexually starved."

Leila Jevons uttered a faint moo of protest; Mary Waterhouse merely smiled tolerantly.

"Don't tell the Duffer, that's all, Leila," added Miss Crimp, with a slight wink. "We don't want any blood shed over you."

"Elsa, don't be so *absurd*," cried Miss Jevons, turning, to her companions' gratification, bright pink.

"Has he...yet?" asked Miss Waterhouse with interest.

"Of course he hasn't."

The entrance of a small boy cut short this promising theme. ("Matron, can I have a clean handkerchief, please? Mr. Wargrave said I was to come and ask for one." "Why did

Mr. Wargrave say that, Wyllie?" "Because he saw me blowing my nose on a dock-leaf, I think, matron. Jolly good things, dock-leaves, when you haven't got a handkerchief, matron." "Where's the handkerchief you had clean yesterday morning?" "I don't know, matron. I think I must have lost it. I can't find it anywhere, matron. Honour bright! P'raps old Posh pinched it, to wipe up Nora's tears, 'cos she won't see him again till next term." "That will do, Wyllie. Here's your handkerchief. Don't lose this one." "Oo, thank you, matron. Don't tell Goggle-eyes, will you?" "That will *do*, Wyllie.")

"What *is* all this about Mr. Parker and Nora?" demanded Miss Crimp, almost before the door had closed. "I'm always hearing references to it."

"Just a silly joke of the boys," Miss Jevons replied, a little absently, for she was wondering how to account to Amy Harrison for Wyllie's missing handkerchief without giving the boy away.

"Yes, but is there anything in it?"

"Of course not," said Miss Waterhouse, looking down her rather pretty nose. "Mr. Parker's the last man to interfere with one of the maids. It's just one of their ridiculous ideas. I believe they use it to try to annoy Sergeant Turner. He and Nora are supposed to be going to make a match of it."

"Posh and the Parlourmaid," meditated Miss Crimp. "Rather a nice title, don't you think? It's astonishing how apt the boys' nicknames are. 'Posh' is exactly the right name for Mr. Parker."

"It's all very absurd," Miss Waterhouse observed severely, "and rather unpleasant."

"But there's seldom smoke without fire," opined Miss Crimp hopefully.

Miss Waterhouse frowned in a pained way. "Sometimes I'm inclined to think, Elsa, that you've got rather a nasty mind."

"Well, that's better than having no mind at all, my dear," retorted Miss Crimp cheerfully.

"Are you ready for some more tea, Elsa?" asked Miss Jevons, with tactless hastiness.

Miss Crimp smiled, and declined another cup of tea. Leaning back in her chair she crossed her rather short legs and introduced the topic which more than any other had engaged the breathless attention of the female side of the Roland House staff during the latter half of the present term. As an abiding source of discussion it could oust even such items of compelling but temporary interest as the Astonishing Behaviour of Mr. Harrison.

"How has Amy been getting on the last few days?" she asked. "Made any progress?" It was not in the least necessary to refer any more specifically to the particular matter in which Amy might have made progress.

"They were walking round the garden together for simply *hours* last night, after supper," reported Miss Jevons eagerly.

"But no definite announcement yet?"

"Not yet."

"She'll have to hurry if she's going to bring it off before the end of the term," pronounced Miss Crimp.

Miss Waterhouse smiled: the rather superior smile of one who has already brought "it" off. And she glanced, as if unconsciously, at the neat ring on the third finger of her left hand.

The other two, plunging at once into their hundredth discussion of Amy's chances, affected to notice neither the smile nor the glance.

Up till the middle of the term it had been impossible to deal adequately with this entrancing topic in the presence of Miss Waterhouse without embarrassment, for during the previous term Mr. Wargrave had, to eyes knowledgeable in such matters, shown distinct signs of being interested in Mary Waterhouse herself; moreover Mary Waterhouse, to those same eyes, had shown equal signs of nourishing and returning such interest. Both were earnest souls, and the feminine side of the staff had been already prepared to sit back and bless the solemn union. Mr. Wargrave was the third master, next in seniority to Mr. Duff and superior only to Mr. Rice; and though the third master in a preparatory school can hardly be considered any great catch, he is undoubtedly better than no catch at all.

This term, however, Miss Harrison had intervened. She had not troubled to hide her intentions. It had been very plain indeed that during the holidays she had thought the matter over, decided to approve of Mr. Wargrave, and now meant to have him; and she had gone about the acquiring of him in her usual direct fashion. She was, in fact, following in mother's footsteps. And whether in consequence of this direct attack or not, it was nevertheless a fact that Mr. Wargrave's attentions to Miss Waterhouse had quite abruptly ceased.

Sympathy was entirely with Miss Waterhouse, who bore her presumed disappointment with fortitude and patience. Miss Crimp indeed had gone so far as to assert that Mr. Wargrave was a Schemer; that having early noticed possible evidences of interest in himself on the part of Miss Harrison, he had deliberately played up the innocent Miss Waterhouse in order to quicken the beating of Miss Harrison's heart; for just as it was indisputable that whoever married Miss

Harrison would one day inherit Roland House, so was it indisputable that Mr. Wargrave was an ambitious as well as an earnest young man.

Miss Waterhouse herself, when this theory had been tentatively hinted to her by the sympathetic but tactless Miss Jevons, had laughed heartily. There had never been anything at all between herself and Mr. Wargrave, she had declared frankly, beyond a certain community of interests, not even the very mildest flirtation; and indeed it was difficult, even for Miss Crimp's agile invention, to imagine Mary Waterhouse flirting. Nevertheless this statement, when reported by Miss Jevons to Miss Crimp, had at once been attributed to Pride, covering a Bruised Heart; it was therefore something of a shock to both her colleagues when Miss Waterhouse, returning from the usual half-term weekend, had announced with modest pleasure that she had become engaged to an Australian sheep-farmer and had at once given notice to leave at the end of the term in order to go out to Australia and marry him. Australian sheep-farmers, Miss Waterhouse had discreetly allowed it to be gathered, are an impatient race.

It was therefore now quite possible to examine in the presence of Miss Waterhouse the chances of Miss Harrison. The opinion was that they were favourable, but that some strenuous work would be required on her part during the present week. Mr. Wargrave, it seemed, was being coy.

IV

To his charges at that moment Mr. Wargrave seemed anything but coy.

Indeed, as Master Allfrey, aged eleven, very pertinently remarked to Master Knox, aged twelve: "I tell you, Groggy, old Stinks is a fair stinker. I'd sooner have Pudden, or even old Posh, any day." An observation which Master Knox rightly interpreted as follows: "Believe me, Knox, Mr. Wargrave is not a pleasant fellow to have in authority over one. I would sooner be in the charge of Mr. Rice, or even Mr. Parker."

One of Mr. Wargrave's habits which had endeared him neither to his colleagues nor his charges was that of improving the hour of the moment, shining or not. It was Mr. Wargrave's custom, for instance, once a week to give voluntary lectures on science in one of the classrooms after prep. in the evening, during the half-hour before bed-time which on the other days of the week was devoted to the purging of those animal spirits which afflict the young. Both masters and boys agreed that this showed altogether too much zeal. Only Amy approved; and Amy's approval resulted in the "voluntary" attendance at the lectures proving very much of a courtesy term.

In vain did the little lads savagely mock among themselves at Mr. Wargrave's solemn mannerisms, his stiff collars and strange ties, his rather pronounced Lancashire accent, his ill-cut clothes, and all the other characteristics which made young Mr. Wargrave the Blighter he was unanimously voted. In vain. Against his earnest intentions for their good they were helpless. With all the strength of his twenty-seven years Mr. Wargrave strove for his charges' good.

And yet, as Master Knox, aged twelve, equally pertinently remarked to Master Allfrey, aged eleven, with just that touch of condescension which his superior year demanded: "Well, my good fool, the beastly stinker isn't a beastly *sahib*, that's why. I've a beastly good mind to write to my beastly people about him. They'd be fair beastly riled if they beastly well knew, I can tell you."

"Now then," said Mr. Wargrave, "stop chattering, Knox and Allfrey, and hurry up with that mortar. We want to get this course laid before changing-time, you know. Get a move on."

Messrs. Knox and Allfrey hurriedly resumed work with their spades.

The work on which they were engaged was another of Mr. Wargrave's admirable schemes for teaching the young the Useful Things of Life. ("Though what use it's going to be unless we're all going to be beastly bricklayers I'd beastly well like to know," as Master Knox was wont to observe with some bitterness.) He had propounded it to Mr. Harrison earlier in the term, and been met with Amy's full approval. Since then, and in their spare time, the school had most unwillingly built a low wall across the bottom of Mr. Harrison's lawn where before only a wire fence had stood to divide it from the paddock beyond. What irked them chiefly was that the really interesting job of actually laying the bricks had been annexed throughout by Mr. Wargrave; theirs only the soul-destroying jobs of mixing the mortar, fetching, carting, and carrying, and acting generally as bricklayers' labourers. Nor had their gloom been lessened by the contemptuous snorts of Mr. Parker as he passed them, the benevolent observation of Mr. Harrison, who appeared callously delighted at getting his wall built for nothing beyond the cost of materials, or the open jeers of Mr. Rice.

At first it had been good fun. Mortar can be made the most amusing stuff. A dollop of it shoved down young

Williams's back, or rubbed in Haddon Hall's hair, or thrown surreptitiously at Adye so that it lodged most humorously in his mouth, was without doubt capable of making its recipient look a perfectly beastly fool. But Mr. Wargrave had no sense of humour. He had stopped all such attempts to leaven labour with a little innocent fun in the most heavy-handed way. By the end of the term the whole school was vowing, with bitter unanimity, that they would never have anything to do with the building of a brick wall again as long as they lived. Mr. Wargrave, it must be admitted, belonged to the type of schoolmaster that is made but not born. Practically all schoolmasters do.

Muttering naughtily beneath their breaths, Messrs. Knox and Allfrey began with moody spades to turn over what remained of the pile of mortar. The knowledge that Miss Harrison had come out of the house and was now eyeing them in her usual gimlet way, did not alleviate their depression.

"*Cave*—Goggle-eyes," whispered Master Allfrey to Master Knox, whose back was towards the newcomer; and immediately Master Knox's back began to be afflicted by a strange feeling, as if a series of neat little holes were being punched in it up and down his spine.

Amy turned to Mr. Wargrave with a slight frown. Not even her intentions towards him could interfere with her duty. "Do you think it wise to put Knox and Allfrey at any job together? They encourage one another, you know."

A lesser one than Mr. Wargrave would at once have dislodged from the mortar-heap either Knox or Allfrey. He did nothing of the sort. He merely said, a trifle shortly: "I put them there together on purpose. I intend them to encourage one another. I'm waiting for them."

Amy looked at him in admiration.

V

Mr. Rice had changed, and was knocking a ball against one of the brick walls which bounded Mr. Harrison's tennis-court. From one side to the other he bounded gracefully, keeping the ball continually in play with deft strokes. The windows of one side of the house, and actually of Mrs. Harrison's bedroom, looked down on the court; and one never knew.

Out of the corner of his eye he saw a slender, white-clad figure approaching across the court. She hailed him, and as if with a start of surprise he despatched the ball towards a clump of bushes that stood in a corner, surrounding a summer-house.

"Clumsy!" called out Mrs. Harrison gaily.

Mr. Rice smiled. "You made me jump. Never mind. I'll get it." He went into the summer-house.

A moment later his voice floated out from it. "I say, this is rather funny. Come and see where it's lodged."

Phyllis Harrison went into the summer-house.

"Where is it? I don't see it."

"Nor do I. But it was a good idea, wasn't it?"

Mrs. Harrison laughed happily.

"Darling!" observed Mr. Rice, and took her in his arms.

An assistant master at such a hole as Roland House, Mr. Rice held, is entitled to any amusements he can get.

CHAPTER VI

I

THE TIME WAS NOW TEN MINUTES TO TWO, AND A FINE summer afternoon. Outwardly all was peace, and even love. Miss Waterhouse, for instance, loved and was beloved; Mrs. Harrison loved, and thought herself beloved; even Amy Harrison was exuding by the wall something in Mr. Wargrave's direction which might pass for love, tempered with common sense, though still not quite sure what she was getting back in return. Everything, in fact, for a preparatory school nearing the end of its longest term, was on the surface almost too good to be true. But only on the surface. Underneath it deep currents ran wickedly. Only a splash was needed to bring them into action.

The splash was duly supplied, by a certain Jenkinson major. It was as if Jenkinson major had hurled a large rock into the placid pool of that afternoon, so that from its impact circling eddies swept out, one after another in ever-increasing orbits till they had rocked and shaken everything within sight.

Jenkinson major intercepted Mr. Rice as he left the tennis-court, having hung about for over twenty minutes for that purpose, and said: "Sir, please, sir, did you know, sir? I can't play in the match this afternoon, sir."

"What's that?" frowned Mr. Rice. Jenkinson major was the best bat in the school. His presence in the Green team had had to be counterbalanced by an adroit arrangement of the rest of the batting strength in the other teams. "What's that? Not ill, are you?"

"No, sir."

"What's up, then? If it's matron…"

"Please, sir, it isn't matron, sir. It's Mr. Parker, sir. He's kept me in, sir."

"What!" thundered Mr. Rice.

In delighted terror Jenkinson major explained. Mr. Parker had said his Virgil paper that morning had been a disgrace to the form, a disgrace to the school, a disgrace to the massed preparatory schools of England. He had to stop in that afternoon and work through it with books.

"It's rather a shame, sir, isn't it? Considering the match, I mean, sir. I thought I'd better tell you, sir, in case you wondered where I was, sir."

"Go and change, Jenkinson," said Mr. Rice, with compressed lips. "*I* will speak to Mr. Parker."

"Yes, sir, thank you, sir," squeaked the delighted Jenkinson, who had counted upon that very outcome, and rushed off to spread the joyful news that old Pudden wasn't half in a hairy bate and was going to tick old Posh off to hades.

Mr. Rice strode into the masters' sitting-room. His very tread thumped out such fury that after one startled glance, Mr. Duff shot into cover behind the *Daily Express* and remained there during the whole interview.

"Look here, Parker," said Mr. Rice, in the voice of one who has stood about as much nonsense as he intends to stand. "Look here, Jenkinson major's just told me that you've kept him in this afternoon. There's some mistake, of course."

Mr. Parker, who had been waiting and not without some trepidation for this moment ever since lunch, lowered *The Times* and prepared for battle. "There's no mistake. Why should there be?"

"Well, you can't keep him in this afternoon."

"I can and I have kept him in this afternoon."

"But it's the league final."

"Indeed?" said Mr. Parker coldly. "I'm afraid I can't help that."

"The match will be a farce without him."

"I'm sorry," said Mr. Parker, without truth, and picked up *The Times* again.

"Damn it, man, keep him in some other afternoon. To-morrow if you like, but—"

"Is there any need to swear about it, Rice?"

"Oh, don't be such an old fool!"

They eyed one another stormily. Mr. Parker began to breathe in heavy little snorts.

Mr. Rice forced a smile. "Anyhow, no need to lose our tempers about it. He ought to be kept in, of course. I quite see that. But not this afternoon, you see. It'll only spoil the match for all the rest, which naturally you don't want to do. Do you?" He supposed that the old idiot must be humoured.

"I'm exceedingly sorry if the match will be spoiled," returned Mr. Parker with ponderous dignity, still breathing heavily, "but I'm afraid I have no alternative."

"But damn it, man—"

"I'd really be obliged if you wouldn't swear, Rice."

"You know perfectly well you did it on purpose," roared Mr. Rice, with new fury. "You wanted to spoil the match."

"I don't understand you. His Virgil paper was a disgrace."

"Damn his Virgil paper!"

"And damn your infernal professional leagues!" suddenly shouted Mr. Parker.

"I'll go and see Harrison! You're jealous. That's what you are—jealous!"

"You can go to hell!"

Mr. Duff cowered as if it was lightning that had been playing round him. He knew it was all very childish, and yet it did not seem childish in the least.

II

At this point Mr. Rice had the game in his hands. If he had gone straight from the masters' sitting-room to Mr. Harrison, which actually meant to Amy, for by this time Amy had joined her father in his study, Mr. Parker's defeat was assured. Mr. Parker was an Inefficient, and it was Amy's habit to side automatically against the Inefficients, right or wrong. Where Mr. Rice made his capital mistake was in forcing Amy, vastly against her will (which of course made her all the more angry), into Mr. Parker's camp.

The insignificant cause of this strange alliance was the

person of one Purefoy, who, encouraged by the story of Jenkinson major, was lying in wait for Mr. Rice in the neighbourhood of the masters' sitting-room.

"Sir, please, sir!" bleated Master Purefoy.

"Go away," said Mr. Rice.

"Sir, Jenkinson major said I'd better tell you, sir."

The name of Jenkinson major brought Mr. Rice up short. "Well?"

"Sir, I can't play in the match this afternoon, sir."

"What!" roared Mr. Rice. "Do you mean to say Mr. Parker...?"

"Sir, no, sir. I'm not in his form, sir. Miss Harrison said I wasn't to play, sir."

Mr. Rice regarded the boy. Purefoy was the school's star fast bowler. Had he been in the Yellow team his absence that afternoon would not have mattered so much, for it would have neutralised to some extent that of Jenkinson major. But he was not. He was in the Green team. The Green team consisted in fact of Jenkinson major and Purefoy. There were nine rabbits as well, but they did not count. Without Jenkinson major the Greens were only half a side. Without Jenkinson and Purefoy they were no side at all.

"And why," asked Mr. Rice with deadly calm, "did Miss Harrison say that you were not to play this afternoon, Purefoy?"

"Sir, she said I've got a cold, sir," squeaked Purefoy indignantly. "Just because I happened to sneeze, sir, only once, sir, when she—"

"That'll do. Have you got a cold or not?"

"No, sir, I haven't, sir."

"Then go and change," ordered Mr. Rice.

In high delight Master Purefoy scuttled away. He had a tale to cap even Jenkinson's. Old Pudden was fair on the war-path. He was going to put it across old Goggle-eyes now as well as old Posh.

Mr. Rice strode on. With barely a courtesy knock on the door he strode into Mr. Harrison's study, where Amy was engaged in telling her unfortunate parent a good deal about himself that he had only remotely suspected, and more still that he had not suspected at all.

He welcomed his junior master's intrusion. "Ah, Rice," he said. "You want to see me? Amy..."

"I should prefer Miss Harrison to stay," replied Mr. Rice, very formally and correctly.

Mr. Harrison blinked at him. People seldom wanted Amy to stay when there was a good chance of getting rid of her.

"Yes?" he said.

Mr. Rice detailed his grievance about Jenkinson major.

Mr. Harrison, looking distressed, made deprecatory noises. Mr. Parker was his senior master. It was impossible to have senior masters overridden by junior ones. Mr. Parker was almost a friend of the family. It was impossible to indulge friends of the family at the expense of reason and justice. Mr. Harrison found it all very difficult.

As usual when things were difficult he looked at Amy.

Amy drew down her sparse brows and prepared to deliver the official verdict. It was at this point that Mr. Rice threw the engagement away.

"And by the way," he said loudly, "I met Purefoy just now. He said you'd told him he couldn't play because he's got a cold. He hasn't got a cold at all. I sent him off to change."

"You—sent him off to change?" Amy gasped. "When—"

"There's too much coddling in this place," pronounced Mr. Rice, still more loudly. "Even if he had got a cold, which he hasn't, you don't imagine it's going to hurt him to play cricket on a hot day like this? Just the thing for a cold. Don't want to make mollycoddles of the boys, do you?"

Mr. Harrison listened aghast. Not ever before had he heard such robust words addressed to his daughter.

Amy herself was no less aghast. A moment before she had actually been sympathising with this insufferable young man—had been thinking that Mr. Parker was a jealous old fool, trying to put a particularly mean spoke in his rival's wheel, and that it was high time that a firm stand was taken. Now she saw she had been wrong. It was indeed time a firm stand was taken, but not against Mr. Parker. Amy now saw quite clearly that Mr. Parker was not a jealous old fool at all, but a singularly far-sighted man who recognised insufferableness when he met it and knew how to deal with it. Mr. Parker bounded up so high in Amy's estimation that he became almost unrecognisable.

"You sent Purefoy off to change?" repeated Amy wonderingly. "Mr. Rice…"

"Well?" said Mr. Rice aggressively.

"I never heard such a piece of impertinence in my life," said Amy, with another incredulous gasp.

Mr. Rice turned a fiery red. "Impertinence! Well, I'll be… I came here to complain to your father of *your* impertinence. I'm the games master, aren't I? How dare you order a boy not to play cricket without reference to me?"

"How *dare* I…?" choked Amy. "In my own school…"

"Your father's school," corrected Mr. Rice loudly. "Good God, anyone would think you owned the place."

"Father!" cried Amy shrilly.

"I can tell you, everyone's getting a bit sick of it," shouted Mr. Rice, "and it's about time someone said so to you."

"*Father!*"

The door opened, and Phyllis Harrison came in. She glanced from red face to red face in amazement, and then at her husband, who, apparently petrified, sat clutching the edge of his desk.

"What on earth is going on?" asked Mrs. Harrison with interest. "A glee competition, or something?"

"Oh, nothing," muttered Mr. Rice.

"My dear," bleated Mr. Harrison, looking like a goat in distress, "I think perhaps you had better…"

"Are you having a row?" enquired Mrs. Harrison, with still more interest, and, disregarding her husband's feeble attempt to get rid of her, perched her white-clad form on the arm of a chair and regarded the combatants with approval. "Go on. Don't mind me. Who's winning?"

Mr. Rice thought he saw a chance. He threw off his fiery hue and addressed his late tennis-pupil in the formal tones of the junior master towards his headmaster's wife.

"It's really a matter that concerns you, Mrs. Harrison, if you'll allow me to put it."

"Me?" smiled Phyllis. "Good gracious. Were you quarrelling with Amy about me?"

"Certainly not. I meant that the point of our—discussion is really your concern, you being responsible for the boys' health here."

"Am I?" asked Phyllis doubtfully, with a glance at her

fuming step-daughter. It was a point on which she had never been at all sure.

"Well, of course," replied Mr. Rice, with a faint air of surprise. "Miss Harrison saw fit just now to issue an order on your behalf, which I personally thought was a mistaken one. That was what we were talking about. I should like to put the point to you." He did so.

"Not very difficult, is it?" said Mrs. Harrison lightly, when he had finished. "Has the boy got a cold or has he not? One sneeze doesn't make a cold, you know."

"No, he hasn't," said Mr. Rice.

"Yes, he has," snapped Amy, who had gone into a cold fury and yet found herself helpless before these tactics.

The confidential smile which her father's wife directed towards Mr. Rice did nothing to allay her anger.

"And what do you think about it, dear?" cooed Mrs. Harrison, who was enjoying herself and did not mind Amy knowing it. Mrs. Harrison seldom got a chance of enjoying herself at Amy's expense. The six years between their ages did not allow her to exercise any step-maternal authority over her husband's masterful daughter, and yet was enough to prevent the school-girlish repartees which so frequently offered themselves to her lips. Amy also had the annoying habit of making her step-mother usually feel six years younger than herself instead of six years older.

Mr. Harrison, thus unfairly thrust into his proper position, naturally hedged. He was secretly almost as much in awe of his junior master as he was of his daughter.

"Is it really very important that Purefoy should take part in the match, Rice?"

"Just as important as that Jenkinson should," replied Mr. Rice firmly. "Without them, the game will be just a farce."

"I fail to see that that is as important as risking the boy's health," retorted Amy icily. "There's a good deal too much attention being paid to games here at present. One would think that the school existed for nothing else. Mr. Parker is perfectly right. It's nothing but professionalism."

"Perhaps you'd like him to take the games over again," sneered Mr. Rice, "so that the school can go on losing all their matches?"

"I'd sooner see the school lose its matches than its scholarships. It's ridiculous to subordinate games to work. If Jenkinson did such a bad paper, of course he must be kept in to do it again. Mr. Parker was absolutely right. You must agree with me, Father."

"Well," said Mr. Harrison, and pulled at his beard.

"It's a difficult point," said Phyllis with great solemnity, and shook her head. Unfortunately there was a gleam in her eye which neither of the combatants missed.

Mr. Rice went for it boldly. "In any case, I suggest that Miss Harrison is in no position to decide in either case. Purefoy's belongs entirely to Mrs. Harrison, and Jenkinson's to you, headmaster. Will you please give us a decision on Purefoy, Mrs. Harrison?"

"Certainly, Mr. Rice. If as you say, he hasn't got a cold, there's no earthly reason why he shouldn't play."

"Thank you," said Mr. Rice, with dignity. "And about Jenkinson, headmaster?" Mr. Rice always made a point of addressing Mr. Harrison as "headmaster," as in a real school.

"Well," said Mr. Harrison, and again had recourse to his beard.

"If," said Amy through white lips, "I am really as little use here as Mr. Rice suggests, there is no point in my staying till the end of term. You remember that Marjorie Beasley asked me to go and stay with her as soon as term was over, Father. I shall wire her that I am coming to-morrow."

"Amy!" said Mr. Harrison, aghast.

"Amy!" said Mrs. Harrison, no less so.

"Well?" retorted Amy truculently. "You can get the boys off, Phyllis, can't you? I understand it's your job."

"Mr. Rice," said Phyllis, "I'm so sorry. Purefoy can't possibly play this afternoon, with that cold of his."

"Nor Jenkinson," Amy thrust in. "Father!"

"Well, we must certainly pay quite as much attention to our work as to our games," hesitated Mr. Harrison.

Amy delivered the final blow. "Mr. Rice, it isn't my place, as you would be the first to point out, to suggest that you overstepped the bounds not only of your duty but of common courtesy in countermanding the orders of a master senior to you and of myself. I shall therefore leave it entirely to my father to tell you that discipline must be maintained among the staff just as much as among the boys. In the meantime—"

"Headmaster," said Mr. Rice, in a strangled voice, "will you kindly accept my resignation? I shall leave at the end of this term."

"A full term's notice is necessary, I think," replied Miss Harrison coldly. "In the meantime, will you kindly send both Jenkinson and Purefoy back from the field at once."

In the final of the league match that afternoon the Yellows defeated the Greens by an innings and eighty-seven runs.

Mr. Rice was very angry indeed.

His anger was not lessened by the unusual sight of Mr. Parker and Amy hobnobbing in deck-chairs outside the pavilion. Judging from the animation of their talk and the frequent laughter which punctuated it, Amy and Mr. Parker had found a most amusing subject of discussion.

Mr. Rice was not accustomed to being considered amusing. The battle was up.

III

There was a man once who lent his country cottage to some friends. When they came back they thanked him very nicely, and sent him their dirty linen to wash. Mr. Rice was feeling as if Phyllis Harrison had done much the same kind of thing to him.

"But, dearest, you must see I couldn't do anything else," Phyllis explained, with becoming penitence, as she trotted back from the stricken cricket field beside a silently striding Mr. Rice. "I could never have got the boys to their right homes. Really, I couldn't. They'd all have landed up anyhow, with the wrong socks and everything. You must see that."

"You let me down," said Mr. Rice sternly.

"Dearest!" pleaded Mrs. Harrison.

"You made me look a fool with the boys."

"Darling!"

There was a pause.

"Please forgive me," said Phyllis. *"Please!"*

"I shouldn't have expected it of you, Phyllis."

"No, darling. Please forgive me."

"Well, anyhow," said Mr. Rice, with grim satisfaction, "I'm going."

"Oh, you didn't mean it!" Phyllis wailed. "You can't go. Gerald, you can't. Whatever should I do here without you?"

"You've got your husband, haven't you?" retorted Mr. Rice smugly.

Phyllis made a *moue*.

"Well, my dear girl, why did you marry him?"

"Heaven alone knows," said Phyllis frankly. "Won't you take me away with you, Gerald?"

"No, I will not."

Phyllis sighed. "I thought you wouldn't. You don't really love me, do you?"

"Do you really love me?"

"Gerald, of course I do. How can you ask such a thing?" Phyllis's eyes danced towards the large, grim figure at her side. The figure caught them, and Phyllis dropped them modestly. "Would I have…if I didn't love you?"

"Yes," said Mr. Rice uncompromisingly.

Phyllis laughed delightedly. "Gerald, I really do love you when you go so strong and silent and honest. There—you smiled. Not angry with me any more, are you?"

"Yes," said Mr. Rice.

"Say you're not, or I'll kiss you here and now, in front of all the boys. I swear I will. *Are* you angry with me still?"

"No," Mr. Rice said hastily, by no means sure that she was not capable of carrying out her threat.

"That's all right, then," Phyllis said comfortably. "Now, how are we going to get one back on Amy?"

"Really, I haven't the least wish to get one back on Amy."

"Nonsense, darling. Of course you have. Just as much as I have. That's what I love about this place. We're all just as childish as the boys. More, if anything, because we ought to know better. I simply love getting one back on people. I know: I'll go and have a talk with Leila Jevons. Amy tried to get her sacked this morning. She'll be feeling just like we are."

"My dear girl," said Mr. Rice with great dignity, "I assure you I'm not feeling anything."

"Darling!" said Mrs. Harrison fondly.

IV

So all day long the noise of battle rolled.

CHAPTER VII

I

LEILA JEVONS SAT IN FRONT OF HER DRESSING-TABLE, plucking her eyebrows.

Miss Jevons paid a good deal of attention to her eyebrows. Nature had made one or two slips in the designing of them, and Miss Jevons was kept rather busy putting Nature right in the matter. Left to themselves, for instance, Miss Jevons's eyebrows resembled nothing so much as one thick bar extending squarely across the lower edge of her forehead, for it was their habit to meet regrettably across the bridge of her nose. When she was younger Miss Jevons had been accustomed to keep this meeting-place clear by means of a safety-razor, but this had not been altogether a success; the bridge of Miss Jevons's rather puggish nose had been wont at times to bristle like an Arab zareba. The eyebrow-tweezers, though more painful, were infinitely more efficient.

Her eyebrows thinned into two becoming lines, Miss

Jevons pulled her blue cotton kimono absently apart, and leaned forward to examine the wart which had its habitation on the side of her nose. This wart—well, it was not a wart really, if warts have horny crowns, but more of a pronounced mole—was an abiding source of sorrow to Miss Jevons. It had the distressing custom of nourishing three stalwart black hairs, which seemed only to thrive upon constant eradication. Every night Miss Jevons, however tired she might be, spent three or four sorrowful minutes pulling this super-mole this way and that, squeezing it, lamenting over it, and downright tormenting it. Should she have it burnt out or should she not? That was the nightly problem. Would the result be better, or would it be horribly worse? It was a terrible question to have to decide. Miss Jevons had been debating it every night for the last eleven years, ever since she was fifteen, and had not reached a decision yet.

She would have liked, very much she would have liked, to canvass Mr. Duff's opinion on the point. But could one? Would it not be terribly forward? Miss Jevons had a horror of being forward. And might it not frighten him off altogether? On the other hand, might it not offer him the opening which he never seemed able to make for himself? But then again, did he want an opening at all? It was all most difficult.

Miss Jevons rose from her dressing-table stool and, throwing off her kimono, looked at herself in the long mirror. When her mind was harassed and her spirit troubled, as was not infrequently the case, Miss Jevons would always soothe herself by the contemplation of her beautiful legs and wonder whether she would not go on the stage after all.

This evening however Miss Jevons's admiration of her

limbs was almost perfunctory. For once there was so much to think about that even the mole had come off more lightly than usual. Truly it had been a remarkable day. Within a short fifteen minutes that morning she had been dismissed, taken back again, been kissed, and had kissed. Mr. Harrison, of all people…!

Miss Jevons was not prim. She herself was often at some pains to point out, chiefly to Elsa Crimp, that whatever she might be she was not prim. A kiss, one was allowed to gather, meant very little to Miss Jevons. But Mr. Harrison…

True, it had only been on the forehead. Not an exciting kiss by any means. But the point was that it had been a kiss at all from Mr. Harrison. And he had done it so easily, with such practised nonchalance. Could it be that Mr. Harrison was not so stuffy after all? Elsa Crimp had always said that Mr. Harrison was a dark horse; but of course Elsa said that about everyone—even about Mr. Duff. But could it possibly be that Mr. Harrison…? Miss Jevons caught her breath, and forgot her legs and the stage altogether. *Could Mr. Harrison be going to get some of his own back and have selected herself as a partner in the process?*

This was such an exciting conception that Miss Jevons stretched herself on the narrow bed to stare up at the ceiling and think it out.

Had Mr. Harrison tumbled at last to what had been going on between Phyllis and Gerald Rice?

That was the question. Elsa Crimp had thought he had, some time ago, and was only waiting his chance. This had been an exciting, volcanoish idea at first, but Mr. Harrison had now been waiting so long that the excitement had worn thin. It certainly had seemed incredible that Mr. Harrison could have noticed nothing of what had been so plain to the eyes of everyone else, but husbands are notoriously blind, and Miss Jevons herself had come to the conclusion, when nothing happened and nothing happened, that Mr. Harrison had not tumbled. But now…

Suppose Mr. Harrison wanted to begin an intrigue with her…

Regretfully Miss Jevons rose, put on her kimono again, and sat down once more at her dressing-table, to cream her face. She knew perfectly well that the kiss which had been bestowed upon her was not that kind of kiss at all; her imagination had been running away with her, as usual.

Nevertheless she exulted in the fact that it had happened at all. A woman who has been kissed by a man, and only kissed, knows that she has established a claim. Miss Jevons and her old mother were safe now from Mr. Harrison's ruthless daughter.

So now, about Mr. Duff…

About the battle that had taken place that afternoon between Amy and Mr. Rice, Miss Jevons thought very little. She had been used to preparatory schools for nearly five years now, and she could remember no term which had ended without some kind of battle, major or minor. Resignations invariably hurtled through the air during the last few days like hailstones, and yet the resigned ones always turned up again next term smiling as if nothing had happened. Miss Jevons was glad of course that someone had stood up to Amy at last, and she was wholeheartedly on the side of Mr. Rice. And so, she had no doubt, would Mr. Duff be.

Miss Jevons wiped the thick layer of cream off her face, and began to pat the underneath of her chin with a springy shoe-tree.

Yes, and thinking of Mr. Duff...

II

In the small room next to Miss Jevons's small room, Mary Waterhouse had been going through much the same kind of routine, except that she had no mole to bully and her eyebrows were naturally fine and arching, wherefore Miss Waterhouse had the very good sense to leave them alone. And yet Miss Waterhouse was accustomed to spend just as much time in front of her mirror as did Miss Jevons. Perhaps she considered it her duty towards humanity to look her best, which can only be achieved of course in the case of a young woman by spending a great deal of time every night before the mirror. There was, too, in Miss Waterhouse's case her long hair to brush, which more than counterbalanced Miss Jevons's mole and eyebrows.

For Miss Waterhouse wore her fine, dark-brown hair long. Those who knew her well said that she did so because she was that sort of girl. Those who knew her better said that it was because she wished to be thought that kind of girl; but it is a fact that those who know us better do not know us nearly so well, and even if they did would never speak the truth about us. Arguing from facts therefore, all one can determine is that Miss Waterhouse had very beautiful hair which reached below her waist, and that she wore it parted in the middle, dragged uncompromisingly straight back with no hint of wave or curl, and coiled in what are technically known as "snails" over each ear, than which no method of dressing beautiful, fine, long, dark-brown hair could be more unbecoming. But as those who knew Miss Mary Waterhouse well said that she did this thing because she did not care whether she made herself becoming or not, whereas those who knew her better (and on whose knowledge and word it is impossible to rely) said that she did it because she wanted to give just that impression while remaining becoming in her very unbecomingness—well, there seems to be very little argument in it either way.

Certainly one who did not know her at all would not have said that Miss Waterhouse laid herself out to be becoming. Unlike Miss Jevons, she used neither scent nor powder, and lipstick knew her not. She had a somewhat knobbly forehead, which by her style of hairdressing she ruthlessly exposed. Her ears were white and small, yet she hid them. It was obvious that Miss Waterhouse cared not how she looked; and yet she always looked attractive. Her wide mouth smiled slowly, but with charm. Her large, grey-blue eyes at least looked intelligent. She was an excellent listener. What she thought, she had the admirable faculty of keeping to herself. Of all the feminine side of the staff she was at once the most unobtrusive, and the most interesting. She was reputed to be an orphan and entirely dependent on her own capabilities; and no one quite knew what those capabilities were.

Miss Waterhouse was accustomed to devote a whole quarter of an hour every night to the brushing of her hair. She had once read that the conscientious girl will never spend less than a quarter of an hour in brushing her hair, and it was a pity that more girls were not more conscientious. As a conscientious girl Miss Waterhouse therefore knew exactly what to do.

Hair-brushing is to a girl what shaving is to a man, the very best opportunity of the day for thinking out one's problems. Miss Waterhouse had her problems to think out. The present one was what line to take up over this curious business which had arisen between Amy Harrison and Gerald Rice, which threatened to become a good deal more important than the usual end-of-term squabble between two people with frayed nerves. It looked very much as if the whole of the staff was going to be drawn into it before the week was out, to support one combatant or the other; and if that was the case, just what was Miss Mary Waterhouse going to do about it? And that meant, just how could the affair be turned to Miss Mary Waterhouse's advantage? Miss Waterhouse was not one of those foolish virgins who allow their emotions to sway their reason; with Miss Waterhouse reason dictated and emotion fell into line.

To the slow, steady sweeps of her brush she began to forecast the inevitable developments.

On one side already were Amy and Mr. Parker; on the other Mr. Rice and Mrs. Harrison. Both Leila Jevons and Mr. Duff would automatically take anyone's side against Amy, through the instinct of simple protection; almost certainly Mr. Wargrave, if he took a side at all (and it was conceivable that Mr. Wargrave alone of all the staff might not take a side) would range himself under Amy. Elsa Crimp could be depended upon to throw herself into the fray, and on principle against Amy. Neatly Mary saw the sides arranged in her mind like the boys' matches pinned by Mr. Rice on the school notice-board, with Mr. Harrison between the two in the position of umpire.

MR. HARRISON (UMPIRE)

WHITES	COLOURS
Mr. Rice (capt.)	Amy Harrison (capt.)
Mrs. Harrison	Mr. Parker
Mr. Duff	Mr. Wargrave
Leila Jevons	
Elsa Crimp	

Yes, on paper the *Whites* looked the stronger team; but Miss Waterhouse knew that the captain of the *Colours* was worth half a dozen.

About the result there could be no possible doubt whatever.

Without hesitation Miss Waterhouse added herself to the *Colours*.

She would have liked to nominate herself for Assistant Umpire, but saw difficulty in obtaining the agreement of the others, particularly of the captain of the *Colours*.

III

Roland House went to bed early. Mrs. Harrison therefore went to bed, when possible, late. To-night Mr. Harrison would be working late in his study. Mrs. Harrison therefore went to bed early. At the precise moment when Miss Jevons was turning her attention from her eyebrows to her mole, Phyllis Harrison was already taking off her dress.

She undressed slowly, pottering about her bedroom between each garment that she removed, and thinking. Her mind moved in little bird-like hops from one thought to another.

"Gerald and Amy! Whoever would have expected to see a row between those two? What fun!—Dear Gerald… But I do pity his wife, though. I wonder whom he'll marry. And when.—Well, thank goodness I'm safe to-night, at any rate.—Damn! There's a ladder in these stockings. I wish I'd noticed that earlier.—Cecil's working late to-night… Hurrah for the last week of term. But oh, my goodness, the holidays.—Why *did* I marry him? Oh, well, I suppose I might have done worse.—*Would* he be jealous if he knew? Really jealous? I suppose he would, because all men are so possessive, but… Thank goodness I'm not possessive, whatever I may be.— I'm sorry Mary Waterhouse is going. She's a prig, but I can't help liking her. She's useful, too. Amy will miss her.—*Dear* Amy.—Yes, I *do* like this *Mille Et Une Fleurs* scent.

"How I hate this place. Really, sometimes I wish Gerald would take me away. Why *did* I marry Cecil? This isn't the sort of life I ought to be leading at all. I want lights, and music, and witty talk round me. I'm wasted here. Shall I chuck it, and clear out? I wish I could make up my mind. And yet in some queer way I should miss Cecil. Talk about women being mysterious; men are fifty times more so. I've been married to Cecil—what is it? Oh, my gods, four years!—and I don't feel I really know him yet. I know Elsa Crimp thinks he's a dark horse. Perhaps he is. Supposing if he did find out about me and Gerald. Does that frighten me? Yes, it does; it terrifies me—terrifies me, really. And yet I like playing with fire. I *like* being terrified. But what would he do? I wonder. Those weak men—at least, the kind that seems weak in small things of everyday life—when they do take the bit between their teeth they're fifty times worse than the blusterers. Yes, I can see Cecil doing—well, almost *anything*!—Damn, I've got a pag-wamp coming on my cheek. That was the salmon."

Mrs. Harrison then spent five and a half minutes examining her incipient pag-wamp from every possible angle.

She began to cream her face.

"Well, I wish she'd marry him and hurry up about it. Though anyone wanting to marry Wargrave… Well, I suppose an accent doesn't put everybody off. Thank heaven I'm fastidious. I wonder if it really will make her any more human. Marriage ought to, for a woman; but Amy… My goodness, does he realise what he'd be letting himself in for—does he *realise*? Perhaps he does, and that's why she hasn't brought it off yet. But she will. I bet she does. Heaven help the man! No wonder he's got that worried look. *His* number's up.—Bother this pag-wamp. It's going to be a real brute. Just when I wanted to look particularly nice, too. Ah, well, these things are sent to try us, as Mary would probably say. One does one's job. My job will be to look nice in spite of pag-wamps.—Dear Gerald. I really am getting disgracefully fond of that conceited young man. Curse him!—Where's that towel? Oh, why can I never find anything in the place I'm perfectly certain I left it in last?

"Gerald, yes. I must pull his leg about Amy to-morrow. Keep him up to the mark. I'm going to have some gorgeous fun out of this. Well, it's about time I did have a little fun. It's nearly a fortnight since we had that dinner and show in London. A fortnight! My goodness, why did I marry Cecil? Yes, I *know* I might have done worse. But I might have done such a lot better. I wonder if anyone's ever thrown themselves away quite so completely as I have. Well, we shall see; we shall see.

"Oh, curse this pag-wamp!"

IV

Amy Harrison stood at her bedroom door, listening noise-lessly she edged it an inch open, and stood without moving, her ear to the crack. Then an expression of disappointment passed over her face, and she closed the door again. She thought she had heard a movement in the passage upstairs, when no movement should be.

She walked on bare feet across the room and got back into bed, but her ears were still alert. Amy trusted nobody.

In her bed she lay flat on her back, her hands crossed behind her neck, and stared into the dark. She had a good deal of thinking to do, and it was always easiest to think in bed at night.

Mr. Rice's resignation must be accepted. That she had already decided. It was a pity in a way, because he was a real asset to the school, temporary though his stay was. But he had got too big for his boots, and the probabilities were that he could not be reduced again to his correct dimensions; in any case the risk could not be taken. Amy's thoughts played round the scene in her father's study after lunch, and she was annoyed to find that she was still young enough to burn again with anger at the mere memory of Mr. Rice's words and behaviour; she would have liked to be able to recall them only with contempt.

Mr. Rice must go.

Miss Jevons must go.

Somehow Miss Jevons had managed to get round her father that morning, but Amy was not worried about that. With Miss Jevons's person out of the way Amy knew that she could deal adequately with Mr. Harrison. A letter would be sent to that young woman within the first week of the holidays. Amy would see to that. A term's salary would have to be sacrificed, which was a nuisance, but that could not be helped. Miss Jevons would have had to go in any case, as a matter of mere efficiency, but her cajoling of Mr. Harrison that morning made her dismissal for Amy a personal point of honour. So much for Miss Jevons.

Miss Jevons, Miss Waterhouse, and Mr. Rice. Quite a minor exodus. Amy began to turn over the plan that had been forming in her mind during the day. In the darkness her thin eyebrows lowered themselves ominously over her cold eyes. An exodus of any sort is the starting-point. It is easy to turn a minor exodus into a major one.

Amy had almost decided already that now was the heaven-sent opportunity for the purging of Roland House. Now was the time to pluck all weak growths up by the roots and re-plant with the hardy shrubs of efficiency.

Mr. Duff...

Mr. Duff must join the exodus. That was quite certain. Mr. Duff had been at Roland House six years, and it had been six years too long. Mr. Duff was hopeless. He could not teach, he could not keep order, the boys laughed at him openly. Mr. Duff was about as much use in the scheme of Roland House as a split pea. For twenty-four months now Amy had been insisting to her father that Mr. Duff must go, and though

Mr. Harrison had agreed that it was inevitable, Mr. Duff still remained. Now Mr. Duff was going.

How could Mr. Duff be forced out of the place?

That Mr. Harrison could be brought to the point of handing Mr. Duff his dismissal during the few days that remained of the term, Amy did not believe. Mr. Harrison detested dismissing people. Mr. Duff had been in the place six years. That, to Mr. Harrison, seemed to constitute a good enough reason for his remaining there another six. Amy coldly thanked heaven that she was not so soft. What would become of the school if she were? What, indeed?

No, somehow or other Mr. Duff must be driven, or exasperated, or shamed, into resigning. How, Amy had as yet no idea. That must await the inspiration of a future moment.

Elsa Crimp…

Amy did not like Elsa Crimp. That was quite sufficient reason for Elsa Crimp to go. But there were more plausible ones too. Miss Crimp was not a good music teacher, and still less of a good teacher of dancing. Able to play only indifferently herself, and to dance not even so well as that, she had not the gift, as has the born teacher, of imparting more knowledge than she possessed. She did not even bother to try to impart what she had. Laughter and badinage proceeded as a rule from those rooms in which Miss Crimp was supposed to be instructing the young. Laughter and badinage.

Miss Harrison re-knitted her lowering brows. That sort of thing must be stopped.

Music and dancing are not important items in a school's curriculum. It is very doubtful whether parents will even enquire into their offsprings' progress in those subjects. The shortcomings of Miss Crimp had therefore been held hitherto to be outweighed by her advantages. Amy herself had found it extremely useful to be able to say, in those bland, earnest tones which were employed only upon the parents of prospective boarders: "And for music and dancing of course we have Miss Crimp. The daughter of Reginald Crimp, you know. The R.A. Yes, the man who paints those delightful portraits of the Royal Family. Oh, yes, they live in Allingford. Such a charming man. Of course, she has no *need* to do anything; she just can't bear to be idle. Just like her father. Oh, yes, you must meet him. Perhaps if you came to see little Richard you'd come to lunch one day, and I'd ask him. He'd be delighted. He's always in and out of here." That Mr. Crimp, as Miss Harrison well knew, would rather be condemned to paint for the rest of his life without flake-white than go to lunch at Roland House, and had never set foot in the place except once when he came in a towering fury to collect his daughter who had forgotten that the President of the New American Art Club was coming to lunch that day during a brief visit to England, was quite outside the circle.

But now Amy did not like Miss Crimp.

For one thing Miss Crimp was a young woman of character, and Amy had long ago decided that there is room for only one woman of character in a preparatory school. Then it was not at all certain that Miss Crimp, besides being a young woman of character, might not be a young woman of bad character. Amy would not say as much to anyone in the world; would not even hint as much; but really, the things Miss Crimp sometimes said. One cannot be too careful about the tone of a place like Roland House. But in any case

Amy had noticed (and Amy had a sharp eye for that kind of thing) that during this term whenever Amy had had cause to administer some small reprimand to a member of the staff, Elsa Crimp had always been loudly in sympathy with the delinquent. And how can one maintain discipline if that sort of thing is to go on, thought Amy now, with a tightening of her thin lips.

Elsa Crimp must go.

Mr. Parker...

This was going to be awkward. Hitherto Amy had carefully avoided anything that might even remotely be understood as sympathy with any action, word, or thought of Mr. Parker's. Now, owing to the heat of those few minutes in the study, she found herself and her authority committed to his support. But Amy was not the person to allow a small accident like that to blind her to the real facts. Mr. Parker was an incompetent old bungler; by chance, in a rather underhanded attempt to get the better of Mr. Rice, he had put himself in a position in which he had to be supported by authority. Amy was perfectly just. She knew precisely why Mr. Parker had done what he had done, and she knew that Mr. Rice's subsequent indignation, so far as it was directed against Mr. Parker, was perfectly well founded. She knew too that Mr. Parker remained an incompetent old bungler; and therefore Mr. Parker must go.

That was the most difficult of all the tasks that faced Amy. Her father would never give Mr. Parker his *congé*. There was a mist of romance surrounding the burly form of Mr. Parker, encouraged, Amy more than suspected, by Mr. Parker himself. Mr. Parker had been at Roland House as long as Mr. Harrison himself. He had been a junior master under Amy's grandfather. He had nourished a hopeless passion for the first Mrs. Harrison. With acute judgement the first Mrs. Harrison had not chosen him, and Mr. Parker had lived on the fact ever since. Everyone had treated him kindly, the sympathy of Mr. and Mrs. Harrison had enveloped him in a warm cloud, it had been perfectly understood that he was unable to tear himself away from Roland House, he had suffered very visibly; it was all most touching. Mr. Parker had become something of a legend. Not until the advent of iconoclastic Mr. Rice had he been dislodged from a single one of the niches in which he had seated himself so firmly.

Amy was grateful to Mr. Rice. She was not yet sure how the unseating process was to be continued, but now that the lever had once been inserted under Mr. Parker she felt quite competent to handle the other end of it successfully. Mr. Parker was to go.

Next term, Amy was resolved, of the present staff of Roland House there should remain no one but Mr. Wargrave. It would be a grand upheaval, and Amy would have a busy holiday; but it would make things easier all round.

Mr. Wargrave...

Amy's stern young face did not relax in the least; if anything, an expression almost of exasperation passed across it. Well, Amy *was* exasperated. What on earth was the matter with the man? Amy thought she had summed him up quite competently: a determined worker, ambitious, who would marry where hard sense led him, not love. Amy knew quite well that Mr. Wargrave did not love her in the least; no more, in fact, than she loved him. But she had thought that he would have seen at once, just as she had, that they could be of very great service to each other. Ever since her mother died Amy had more or less consciously been looking about for a consort with whom she would share the throne of Roland House; and now that she had decided on one, was the young man so foolish as not to realise his luck? Amy's look of exasperation deepened.

No. She knew Mr. Wargrave. He was not foolish in the least. There was something behind this. Could it be—could it possibly be that he had been so ineffably foolish as to contract some obligation of absurd honour elsewhere? Men were so childish about that sort of thing. She would not have thought Mr. Wargrave one to bother about anything so abstract, but one could never be certain with men.

Well, in such cases frankness paid. She would tackle Mr. Wargrave about it the very next morning. And perhaps that might...

Was that a noise in the corridor upstairs?

Amy jumped out of bed and hurried, a white, avenging angel, to the door.

V

Elsa Crimp sat alone in her drawing-room, smoking a cigarette. At her elbow was a glass of whisky and soda. She did not like whisky, but one owes something to oneself. In the studio at the bottom of the garden her father, under a strong daylight bulb, was putting the high lights on the jewels of a stout merchant-peeress.

Miss Crimp wore an evening dress of bright scarlet velvet,

but in spite of that she looked dissatisfied. One hand ran every now and then through her rather untidy brown hair. She pitched the end of her cigarette petulantly into the empty fire-place. Miss Crimp was in love; and as befits a young and independent woman of to-day, was exceedingly annoyed about it.

But then Miss Crimp really had something to be annoyed about. She was in love with a curate. It was humiliating.

The Rev. Michael Stanford had lived in Allingford for three years now. Miss Crimp had known him for less than one of them. She had met him at Roland House, where he attended for an hour on Monday mornings to take the sixth form in scripture and the catechism, and had fallen in love with him at sight. Miss Crimp was not a person to hide her feelings. By hints less subtle than bludgeon-like, Mr. Stanford had been made aware of the devastation he had wrought. His delight had not been perceptible. Miss Crimp had shared his regrets, but had continued to press her suit.

It was not often that Elsa Crimp consciously took another person for a model. Unconsciously her entire attitude was modelled on that of other persons, chiefly living in Chelsea, but consciously no. Yet Miss Crimp during the last few weeks had had a wistful eye on Amy Harrison. She did not like Amy Harrison; in fact she detested her; but one could not deny that Miss Harrison's methods were effective; it was impossible to imagine that Amy's quarry would escape her in the end, however coyly he might twist and turn during the pursuit. Miss Crimp watched, noted, and went off to do likewise. Nevertheless, Mr. Stanford remained uncaptured. It was a nuisance.

She lit another cigarette.

Mr. Stanford must be compromised, that was all. Hopelessly, irrevocably compromised. But how the devil to compromise a man who turns round and positively runs whenever he sees you coming in the distance? That was the problem.

Her cigarette gave her no help.

She threw it away, and lit another.

Being in love costs a terrible lot in cigarettes.

VI

The Rev. Michael Stanford was brushing his hair. He brushed and brushed at it, polishing his sleek head till it gleamed again. He was thinking of Elsa Crimp.

He was thinking: "I'd sooner die than marry her. But she'll get me in the end. I can't stand out much longer. It's no good complaining to the vicar. He wouldn't understand. He'd laugh. I've told her and I've told her that the celibacy of the clergy is one of my strongest principles. But what does she do? Oh, heavens above, what doesn't she do? I've never met such a girl. It's awful.

"And it's no use leaving here and going somewhere else. She'd only follow me.

"Oh, dear, oh, dear."

He put down his brushes, dropped on his knees by the bedside, and prayed to be delivered from Elsa Crimp.

There was little conviction in his prayer. For the first time since his early teens the Rev. Michael Stanford was beginning to doubt the omnipotence of the Almighty.

VII

In his bedroom at Roland House, Mr. Wargrave smiled complacently at himself in the mirror as he brushed his teeth. He had decided some weeks ago to accept Amy on the last day of term; there were only five days left now.

Mr. Wargrave did not believe in luck. It was not luck that Amy Harrison should, apparently of her own accord, have reached precisely the same conclusion as Mr. Wargrave had reached over two years ago, namely that a marriage between them was the best possible thing that could happen for their joint interests. No, it was not luck in the least; it was sound stage-management; for these last two years Mr. Wargrave had, by the subtlest suggestion, been implanting in Amy's mind just that very idea.

Now Amy of course imagined that the idea was entirely her own, but that was precisely what Mr. Wargrave had intended she should imagine.

Mr. Wargrave was ambitious. For a young master without a degree at either of the major universities, without money, without prospects, without influential friends, and with a slight Lancashire accent, the future may well look bleak. Efficiency at one's job will never lead alone to the proprietorship of a paying school. Mr. Wargrave had known all that from the beginning. He had therefore chosen his school with some care. There had to be an only daughter attached to it, of not too prepossessing aspect. Having found such a school, Mr. Wargrave had dug himself in, made a careful study of the daughter in question and what would be likely to meet with her greatest approval and got to work.

But there was nothing crude in Mr. Wargrave's methods. Amy was never to know the careful plan that had been laid. Amy was never to be in a position to throw up at him that he had married her for her school alone. He was to do no chasing himself; oh, no; Amy was to make the running.

And Amy had made it.

Mr. Wargrave had got a good deal of quiet amusement out of Amy's wooing. It had been such a business-like wooing. There had been no question of love or anything inefficient like that. Amy's wooing had consisted almost entirely in elaborating, clarifying, and throwing back at their own author Mr. Wargrave's original hints. A woman cannot run a boys' school alone, had been the burden of Amy's song, however capable she may be; she must have an efficient male at her side, and that male must be either her brother or her husband, and Amy had no brother. In spite of his habitual earnestness Mr. Wargrave had smiled to himself occasionally, not because he saw the humour of the situation, but because his plan was working out so successfully.

There had been difficulties, of course, but Amy had not known of them. Mr. Wargrave was no celibate, and it is almost impossible for any young man, however earnestly ambitious, to reach the age of twenty-nine without having formed any attachment on the way. Mr. Wargrave's attachment had expected him to marry her. Needless to say, Mr. Wargrave had stood no nonsense of that sort, but there had been the difficulty.

Mr. Wargrave knew he deserved to succeed. With any obstacles in his way he was ready to deal quite drastically.

VIII

Mr. Duff was reading in bed. That is to say, there was a book on his pillow; but Mr. Duff's attention was not really on his book.

Mr. Duff was worried. There was a row going on, and Mr. Duff would be compelled sooner or later to support one side or the other. He wanted to support Mr. Parker and Amy. That was the sensible thing to do. In fact Mr. Duff was quite sure he dared not support any side in opposition to Amy. On the other hand Leila Jevons was already at loggerheads with Amy and would be presumably supporting Mr. Rice's team; and how could Mr. Duff not range himself, obscurely but devoutly, on any side that contained Miss Jevons? It would be hopeless, of course; Mr. Duff knew that; but perhaps even his unimportant alliance might hearten Miss Jevons a little—if she ever noticed it, which was unlikely enough.

Amy...

Mr. Duff thought of his old mother and very nearly ground his teeth. It was for his old mother's sake that Mr. Duff had borne all these years the scarcely hidden insults and contempt of Amy. If he were to lose his place here, what chance would he ever have of getting another; and what would happen to his old mother then? Sometimes, when Amy had been ruder than usual, Mr. Duff would go so far as to soothe himself to sleep with visions of Amy's death, sometimes in a lingering illness of a highly unpleasant nature, sometimes in an extremely painful accident. Mr. Harrison would never dismiss him, Mr. Duff knew; but he knew just as well that Amy was only biding her time to do so. Occasionally he would feel quite desperate and even try to think out ways of diverting Amy from her purpose, such as saving her life or saving the school or introducing into it three or four titled pupils; but all the time he knew he would never be able to do anything that would win him Amy's regard, or even her reprieve.

Amy...

His old mother...

Miss Jevons had an old mother too. It was another wonderful bond between them.

Miss Jevons...

Leila...

Had she really smiled at him rather particularly when he passed her in the hall yesterday morning? *Had* she? For the hundredth time Mr. Duff debated this important question.

For the hundredth time he decided it. No, of course she hadn't. Why should she? It was ridiculous, preposterous, insane to think that a wonderful girl like Leila Jevons could ever...

"Oh, God," groaned Mr. Duff, "I wish we were *all* dead."

IX

Mr. Parker drew the whisky-bottle towards him and contemplated it fondly before pouring himself out another nip. Really a final one this time; yes, really. He deserved an extra one to-night. Well, he had had an extra two already; this made the third. Well, he deserved an extra three then. That was all right. Yes, certainly he deserved an extra three to-day of all days.

Made things right with that damned Amy, and brought

about the resignation of the insufferable Rice. That was a day's work if you liked. An extra three? Dammit, an extra four.

Mr. Parker took his extra fourth.

The house, with the exception of Mr. Parker, slept.

Mr. Parker toasted them with an extra fifth.

PART III

CHAPTER VIII

"And that's as far as you got, Mr. Sheringham? That's a pity. It was just getting interesting."

"It was getting boring to me," said Roger, "and that's why I gave it up."

It was the evening after Moresby's call at the Albany, and once again the two were sitting in front of Roger's fire. The chief inspector had come round with the expressed intention of learning what more he could.

"And have you spotted the victim, sir?"

Roger took a pull at his tankard. "I don't know that I have. As I told you, I can't guarantee to have collected all the wheels within the wheels. Probably a lot more was going on than I ever suspected."

"As it is I was surprised that they hadn't all murdered each other by the end of the week."

"Moresby," said Roger seriously, "if preparatory school terms went on one week longer than they do, the mortality would be tremendous."

"I can quite believe it, sir. I've learnt a lot from that manuscript of yours. So you won't have a guess at who the girl was?"

"Oh, I'll have a guess. It ought to have been Amy, of course. Anybody might have murdered her. I was quite ready to do so myself, after only a couple of weeks, and she was amiability itself to me. But I'm quite sure no one would have had the courage. No, it certainly wasn't Amy. That sort of person simply doesn't get murdered.

"The Leila Jevons type does, though. But what was the motive? She was harmless enough. So far as I know nobody was in the least interested in her personally, except Duff; and he certainly didn't want to murder her. No, I can't think it was Leila Jevons.

"Phyllis Harrison? Well, I've never seen a more obvious affair in progress than between her and Rice. Her husband had motive enough. And you know what those weak men are. When the worm does turn, he very often turns a good deal too far. And yet... Well, I don't know, but Harrison didn't really seem to care enough for her. All wrong, you'll say, in the case of a young wife and a middle-aged husband, but he didn't. And he was a bit afraid of her, I should say. She had a pretty sense of humour, you know, and wasn't nearly such a fool as it pleased her to pretend; bone-lazy, and utterly self-centred of course, but no fool. Not that that would have saved her if Harrison lost his head and saw red, but—"

"There was nothing like that, Mr. Sheringham. It was premeditated if a murder ever was."

"Then it wasn't Phyllis Harrison," Roger said promptly. "The only person who could have planned murder against her was Rice, if she wouldn't give him up. But she would have,

I'm sure. She was only amusing herself with him. Rice was a bit of an oaf, you know.

"Whom does that leave? The pretty parlourmaid, Lily? No. Elsa Crimp? Her curate might well have murdered her. But the best curates don't murder, do they? I don't think she was especially objectionable to anyone else. Personally I found her rather amusing.

"And that only leaves Mary Waterhouse. Well, I'm not sure about her. She was the only one of the lot whom I didn't feel I knew inside out. Sometimes I used to think she was genuine, and sometimes I used to think she was an arrant little hypocrite. On the whole I imagine she was. That smugness of hers was rather too good to be true. And if she was a hypocrite there's no saying how far her hypocrisy might not have gone. Let me see, the girl you found was going to have a baby, wasn't she? Well, that fits Mary Waterhouse all right—and she's about the only one it does fit, too. Yes, and that would account for the story about the Australian, and leaving the country at the end of the term. Yes," said Roger excitedly, "and she was the only one, I think, with no near relatives, so there'd be no one to report it if she disappeared. It is Mary Waterhouse, isn't it, Moresby?"

"It is, sir," said the chief inspector, a little disappointed. He had expected Roger to plump for Amy Harrison.

"Humph," said Roger, and looked more serious. "Mary Waterhouse... So she got murdered, did she? It's a bit of a shock, Moresby, to hear of anyone one's known, even so slightly, getting murdered. Murder's so—final."

"To two people, usually," said the chief inspector grimly.

"Any idea who did it?" Roger asked.

"Not to say really, Mr. Sheringham; but I think I've picked up a tip or two from your manuscript."

"You mustn't rely on that too closely, you know."

"Of course not, sir. But—well, I take it most of the references you make are fact? That wall, for instance?"

Roger nodded. "Yes." He was about to say something further when he caught sight of the significant expression on the chief inspector's face. "I say, Moresby, you don't think...?"

"Well, it's a clue, isn't it, sir? I mean, the chap knew how to build right enough. The joints between those bricks on the cellar floor were properly made; no doubt about that. And then there's the matter of the sand and cement. We never could trace where that came from, you know, and yet cement isn't stuff that's usually bought in small quantities."

"You mean, it was brought from the school all ready?"

"I should say that's how it looks to me."

"Yes." Roger considered. "Yes, it does. By Jove!— Wargrave... I never liked the fellow, but dash it all..."

"There's a bit in your manuscript saying that he and the girl had been sweet on each other once, too."

"Yes. Yes, I believe they were supposed to have been. But that doesn't mean anything really. He may only have been using her to bring Amy up to scratch. He was quite capable of it."

"That really was like you wrote it, sir?"

"About Wargrave and Amy Harrison? Pretty well. She was certainly chasing him, and I don't fancy he was unwilling. He was certainly very earnest, and very ambitious."

"And wouldn't stick at much, in your opinion?"

"No," said Roger, a little unwillingly. "No, I don't believe he would."

"Ah," said Moresby.

Roger got up and drew some more beer.

"But look here," he said, as he sat down again, "how do you know it was anyone from the school at all? It needn't have been, need it?"

"Oh, no; it needn't. But I'd take a bet with you, Mr. Sheringham, that it was. She doesn't seem to have had much life outside the school. We've made enquiries. Always spent the holidays in lodgings somewhere, or staying with one of the other girls. Of course, she *may* have spent a bit of them with a man; we haven't been able to check up on her as close as that; but I don't fancy we need look much further than the school. Do you, sir?"

"No, I'm afraid not. But it's a nasty thought that one of those fellows whom I used to feed with must be a murderer. Ugh!"

"Lots of people must have said that in their time, Mr. Sheringham," observed Moresby drily. "There've been lots of murderers."

The two men kept silence for a few moments.

"Well?" said Roger. "Is there any other way I can help you?"

"That book of yours, sir. How were you going on with it?"

"Oh, I don't know. I've got a few rough notes somewhere. The row was to progress. There was going to be some trouble between Amy Harrison and Rice over the swimming-bath, and a quarrel between Leila Jevons and Mary Waterhouse over something or other. Everyone was to get embroiled a little further. But it's of no importance to you. I mean, it wouldn't have thrown any more light on either your problem or on Mary Waterhouse. You'll have to work it now from the other end, won't you?"

"The other end?"

"The cellar. How did Mary Waterhouse come to get into that cellar? Did she walk there? Was she decoyed? Did anyone see her? Did anyone see the man she was with? Is there any connection between her and that house, or between any of the men—well, say Wargrave if you like—and that house? Can you answer any of those questions yet?"

"Not a one," said Moresby cheerfully. "And it's going to be a job to do so. We tried that end before, but didn't get an inch forrader. We may of course now we know who the girl is, but I'm not hopeful. No, it's the school end we shall have to concentrate on, I fancy."

"Beginning by asking Mr. Wargrave to account for his movements during the first week or so of his last summer holidays?"

"Well, perhaps not beginning that way; but I don't think it will be long before we get to that. Not that it's going to help us much, as we can't put the death closer than a week. No one can be expected to account for every minute of a whole week."

"That's very fairly said, for a policeman," Roger approved.

"Oh, we're fairer than some of you amateurs think," grinned Moresby, not to be drawn.

"In other words, you're going to have some difficulty in proving your case?"

"Plenty, sir, I've no doubt. But that's what often happens to us. We know well enough who's the guilty party, but it's not so easy to prove it."

"Yes," said Roger thoughtfully. "And if you don't have a good deal of luck in this case you're not going to prove it at all."

"Oh, we shall prove it right enough, Mr. Sheringham," returned the chief inspector, with professional optimism. "Don't you worry about that."

"I'm not. This is going to be your case entirely. I don't want to be mixed up in it. Have you been down to Roland House yet?"

"Not personally. I'm going to-morrow morning."

"Though there'll only be four of the original lot, I suppose," Roger remarked carelessly. "Still, the others will be easy enough to trace."

"Four?"

"Harrison, Mrs. Harrison (if she hasn't left him), Amy, and Wargrave."

"No, they're all there. All the ones in your book."

For a moment Roger looked surprised. Then he smiled.

"Of course they are. That was foolish of me. If the staffs of preparatory schools left every time they resigned or were dismissed there'd be a general post throughout England at the end of every term."

"Ha, ha," laughed the chief inspector dutifully.

"Amy and Wargrave have brought it off by now, I suppose?"

"They're engaged to be married, yes."

"And Elsa Crimp and the curate?"

"Miss Crimp and Mr. Stanford are also engaged," said Moresby gravely.

"And Leila Jevons and Mr. Duff?"

"Are not engaged."

"Then you might do a kind action for a change and push them into one another's arms while you're down there, Moresby. You've had enquiries made already, I see?"

"Well, of course, Mr. Sheringham," retorted the chief inspector with dignity. "Seeing you weren't going to help us out this time, we thought we'd better go ahead on our own."

Roger laughed. "Have some more beer, Moresby."

"Well, sir," said Moresby, as if in some surprise at himself, "I don't mind if I do."

CHAPTER IX

As he had said to Roger, Chief Inspector Moresby was fairly satisfied in his own mind that he had the right person under suspicion. Murders in real life are seldom complicated. Where an overpowering motive exists, there, almost invariably, is your guilty party. Assuming, in this case, that Wargrave was the father of Mary Waterhouse's unborn child, the motive was about as strong as could be imagined.

Moresby had said nothing to Roger on the matter, but Miss Waterhouse's past had been of considerable interest. The hospital report on the plate on her fractured leg, which had established her identity, had actually come from a prison infirmary. Mary Waterhouse, known then as Mary Weller, had slipped and fractured her leg on a slippery pavement in trying to escape arrest for stealing another girl's handbag. Her record showed that there were two previous convictions against her, both for small offences. In all, she had served eight months in prison.

It had not been easy to trace the Mary Weller who had

been released from Chester Gaol to the Mary Waterhouse at Roland House three years later. There were no further police-records concerning her. After leaving prison that time the girl seemed to have made a real effort to go straight. Gradually Moresby and the tireless officers under him had uncovered the trail. As a waitress in a café here, as a student at a certain college of shorthand-typing, as a clerk in this office, as a more trusted clerk in that, as the manageress of a small frock-shop in Shaftesbury Avenue, Miss Waterhouse (Waterhouse only in the two last-named situations) had been laboriously identified, until her final appearance as private secretary at Roland House.

Moresby thought he could guess well enough what had happened there. Established now in a well-paid posi-tion, among people who knew nothing of her past, Miss Waterhouse had been anxious to set the final seal of marriage upon her respectability. A mind once crooked never becomes wholly straight. It had probably seemed to her, since no man came forward voluntarily, quite an ordinary thing to trap one. Mary Waterhouse played her cards, as she thought, cunningly enough. Unfortunately, however, she had picked on a man whose ambition was stronger than the feelings of shame and decency which he should have had; and it was ironical, the chief inspector reflected, that she had probably picked him because of that very ambition of his. And as if that was not mistake enough she had picked at the same time perhaps the one man in England who, when she threatened blackmail as she undoubtedly did if marriage was not forthcoming, was prepared actually to shoot her in furtherance of that ambition of his. Thus, at any rate, Moresby's reconstruction.

The enquiries made at Roland House so far had been non-committal. It had not been divulged that Miss Waterhouse and the dead girl found in the Lewisham cellar were the same person. Moresby wished to see for himself the reactions which this piece of news would provoke.

At eleven o'clock on the morning after he had returned Roger Sheringham's manuscript, he was ringing the bell at Roland House.

He asked for Mr. Harrison, without giving his name and business, and was shown into an obvious parking-room for parents. The time of year being now towards the end of March, the Easter term was nearly over and, from what he had learned about preparatory schools from Roger's manuscript, Moresby knew that tempers should now be ragged and nerves on edge. He was callous enough to be pleased that it should be so. Well-controlled nerves on the part of the interviewed are little use to the interviewer.

The door opened and a young woman came in: a young woman with sandy eyebrows and distinctly prominent greenish eyes. Moresby looked at her with interest. Without doubt this was the formidable Miss Harrison.

She smiled on him. There is nothing like the prospect of a pupil for withdrawing the sting from the proprietor of a school.

"How do you do?" she said, coming forward. "I must introduce myself—Miss Harrison. You asked for my father? He's engaged just at present. So perhaps you wouldn't mind telling me what you wanted to see him about. Was it about a boy?"

"No, madam," Moresby said bluntly. "It wasn't about a boy."

"Oh," Amy looked surprised for a moment. When she

spoke again her manner had undergone a complete change. Moresby smiled to himself. "What is it, then?" she asked, quite sharply. "As I said, my father's exceedingly busy. I can deal with any matter for him."

"Not with this one, I'm afraid, madam. I must see your father himself. My business is important. I am a police officer. Here is my card."

Amy scrutinised the card. "Well, really!"

Without appearing to do so, Moresby was watching her closely. Her manner showed nothing but a rather annoyed surprise; not the faintest trace of apprehension was discernible. Well, he thought, she's got no idea; he's dropped her no hint.

"Very well," she said shortly. "I'll tell my father."

Moresby was left alone again.

A few minutes later a maid arrived to conduct him to the headmaster's study. Moresby noted, with inward amusement, that not being a parent he was clearly of no further importance in Amy's eyes.

Mr. Harrison rose somewhat irresolutely from his desk, pulling nervously at his beard and glancing from the card in his hand to his visitor and back again. "You wanted to see me…?"

Moresby waited until the door was closed, and then went to the point bluntly. "I'm sorry, sir, but I have some rather shocking news for you."

Mr. Harrison blinked. "For me?"

"Yes. You remember that girl who was found under the cellar floor in a villa in Lewisham? The papers were full of it. Well, I'm sorry to have to tell you that she has been traced to this establishment."

"To—here? But we haven't—er—lost anyone," said Mr. Harrison stupidly.

"You had a young woman here last summer who went under the name of Mary Waterhouse?"

"Mary Wa—Good heavens, you don't mean...?" Mr. Harrison sat abruptly back in his chair and stared up at the chief inspector, his mouth drooping foolishly open. (It's a good job those parents can't see him, Moresby thought.)

"I'm afraid so, sir. There's no doubt about it."

"But... Why, but she was going to Australia. To be married. She told us so."

"She didn't go."

"But how do you know? Have you looked...?"

"In Australia?" said Moresby patiently. "No, sir. There's no need. I can't go into details at this stage, but you can take it from me quite definitely that there's nothing wrong with the identification. And that being the case I want to ask a few questions about her life here, if you'd be good enough to answer them."

"Yes, yes," muttered Mr. Harrison, and pushed a bell-push on his desk with a finger that visibly shook. "Yes, of course. But I can't believe... Yes, of course." In reply to an obviously interrogatory glance from Moresby at the bell-push he added: "I'll send for my daughter. We'd better have her in. She'll know far more about Miss Waterhouse than—er—than I do."

"Very well, sir," Moresby assented affably. To himself he was thinking: Mr. Sheringham hit this old bird off all right. And the girl. Wonderful how these writers do it.

The maid who answered the bell was sent off in search of Miss Harrison, and Moresby filled up the interval before her appearance with putting one or two questions about Miss Waterhouse's duties. Mr. Harrison, however, seemed to be becoming with each moment more horror-struck at the fate which had overtaken his late secretary, so that his answers grew more and more mumbled. Finally Moresby gave him up, and frankly waited for his daughter.

"Yes?" said that young woman brusquely to her father, taking no notice of Moresby on the hearthrug. "What is it, Father? I'm very busy."

"My dear, that nice girl who was here last summer…your secretary…you remember."

"My secretary?"

"Yes, yes. Miss… Miss…"

"Waterhouse," put in Moresby.

"Waterhouse, yes. As I was saying. Miss Waterhouse… you remember?"

"Of course I remember. What about her? She went to Australia, to get married. Or so she said. She's never written. Why? Are the police after her?"

"The police have found her, Miss Harrison," Moresby replied, for the force. "She's dead. Murdered."

"Indeed?" Amy stared at him coldly through her rimless pince-nez.

"You remember the girl found under the cellar floor in that villa in Lewisham? That was Miss Waterhouse."

"Nonsense," said Amy crisply. "I don't believe a word of it."

"That," said Moresby gently, "unfortunately does not alter the fact of Miss Waterhouse having been murdered, Miss Harrison."

It took a minute or two to persuade Miss Harrison that

someone known to her had actually had the bad form to get herself murdered, and Moresby then went ahead with his questions. At first he began by putting these as much to Mr. Harrison as to his daughter. Since, however, Amy answered each one, and Mr. Harrison could only pull his beard distractedly and mutter into it, the nominal head of the establishment was soon relegated to the background, where he remained practically ignored. In any case he seemed to prefer it so.

Even Amy, however, was not very helpful, but Moresby was satisfied that this was because she could not be, not because she was keeping anything back. Miss Waterhouse had answered an advertisement for a personal secretary in the first place; her references were excellent, she herself had made an admirable impression; Amy had engaged her at once. With her usual efficiency Amy had made notes of the references in question, which she was now able to produce; two of them were from the two last firms with whom Miss Waterhouse was known to have worked; the third, and most glowing, must have been forged. Since her engagement Miss Waterhouse had given complete satisfaction. She was neat, methodical, and willing in her work; with the infants' class, in which type of work she had frankly stated at the beginning she had had no experience whatever, she had proved an excellent governess; she had been popular with the rest of the staff; Miss Harrison had been very sorry to lose her.

On the question of her relations with Wargrave, Moresby purposely did not touch, except to ask, with apparent jocosity, how it was that such a paragon had not made a hit with any impressionable junior master; to which Amy coldly retorted that that kind of thing was not encouraged at Roland House, and in any case Miss Waterhouse had quite evidently not been that kind of girl.

"I see you don't remember all the details of the case, Miss Harrison," Moresby replied. "You're forgetting that the girl who was found, Miss Waterhouse, was going to have a baby. Can you account for that in any way?"

Miss Harrison's sallow face flushed. "I cannot. And even if I could, I should prefer not to do so. In any case, I never repeat scandal."

"Ah, there was some scandal, then, connected with Miss Waterhouse?" Moresby said quickly.

"None, so far as I know. My remark was a purely general one."

"I see. Then although this may be the motive for the death of a friend of yours, whom you liked and respected, you won't tell me anything which might help us to find out who killed her?"

But Amy was not to be caught by those methods.

"I'm afraid it isn't a case of 'won't,'" she answered calmly. "I simply don't know anything. If I did I would tell you, whoever was involved. One has one's standards."

Moresby believed that she was speaking the truth.

He asked Mr. and Miss Harrison to keep all this news to themselves at any rate until he had interviewed the various members of the staff, explaining that he wanted to come on each mind fresh before opinions, possibly erroneous, had had time to crystallise, and enquired laboriously as to names.

"You'd better see them in order of seniority, if you really want to question each one," Amy said briskly, having run through the list. "I'll send for Mr. Parker."

"Mr. Parker? Ah, yes; the senior master, isn't he? Well, I think I won't see him first after all. It would be better to keep him to the end, I fancy, in case anything crops up from the others that I might want him to check. I think I'll begin with one of the junior ones. Let me see, you said they were...?"

"Mr. Wargrave and Mr. Rice."

"Ah, yes. I'd forgotten. I'll begin with Mr. Wargrave, then. Now, that was a very handy little room where you saw me first, Miss Harrison. Do you think I might have the loan of that, for these interviews?"

"Certainly. I'll ask Mr. Wargrave to come to you at once. Father, just take Mr... er..."

"Don't bother, please, Miss Harrison." Moresby had already rung the bell for the maid. "I couldn't give you the bother of fetching Mr. Wargrave yourself. We'll just send the maid for him, because I've remembered another couple of questions I wanted to ask you."

He hurriedly thought up one or two unimportant queries, and invested them with as much solemnity as he could. Moresby was taking no chances. Sure though he was in his own mind that Amy Harrison knew nothing, he was not going to risk the conveyance of any sort of warning to Wargrave.

Two minutes later he was conducted, by Mr. Harrison, across the hall into the morning-room, where Wargrave was waiting for him. With a muttered word or two instructing the latter to answer any questions that were put to him, Mr. Harrison left them together.

Moresby sized up his man in a swift glance: the rather narrow forehead, pinched together on the temples, on which the hair grew low, the big jaw and determined mouth, the slightly snub nose, the large and protuberant ears, the closely-cut hair, the eyes, set just a little too close together and surmounted by heavy, black brows, the general build below medium height but stocky and powerful, the large hands. A difficult, sulky-looking customer, decided Moresby, and no mistake, and not one who looked likely to give anything away.

He assumed his most genial expression.

"Mr. Wargrave?"

"Yes?"

"I am a police officer, from Scotland Yard."

Mr. Wargrave raised his formidable eyebrows a fraction of an inch, but said nothing.

Moresby pushed his hands in his pockets. "I've come on a highly unpleasant errand, Mr. Wargrave; and though I know everyone here will give me all the help they can, the bringer of bad news is never welcome, is he?" Moresby smiled.

Mr. Wargrave did not return the smile. "You mean, someone's been getting into trouble?" he asked, and Moresby noticed the Lancashire accent in his voice.

"Somebody's got, sir. You remember a Miss Waterhouse who was here for about a year, up till last summer?"

"Very well. She went to Australia."

"Excuse me, sir, she didn't. She went to Lewisham, and *somebody* murdered her there."

Moresby had purposely conveyed the information with as much brutal bluntness as he could. Moreover, by putting a little extra stress on the word "somebody" he conveyed just the faintest hint that the identity of that "somebody" was perfectly well known to himself.

The result was disappointing.

"Oh!" said Mr. Wargrave, and added nothing further. His expression did not alter by a fraction.

"You don't seem very surprised, sir?"

"On the contrary," returned Mr. Wargrave imperturbably, "I am extremely surprised. How did it happen?"

"You remember the Lewisham Basement Mystery, as the papers called it?"

"Oh! So that was—Miss Waterhouse?" Wargrave turned suddenly away, and fiddled with the window.

"It was."

There was a moment's silence.

When Wargrave spoke again his words were perceptibly more hesitating. "Have you any idea who—did it?"

"That's what I'm here for, sir, to try to find out."

"You think the answer lies here, then?" Wargrave asked sharply. "That's ridiculous, of course."

"I can't say. It may be, and yet again it may not. But she'd been here up to within a week or two of her death, so it's here that I've got to start my enquiries. So if you'll be good enough to answer my questions, sir—" With a business-like air Moresby produced a note-book and pencil.

But the questions he put were only general ones. Not even by an inflection of the voice did he hint at his knowledge that there might have been more between Miss Waterhouse and Wargrave than between her and any other member of the staff. This was not the real interview with Wargrave. That would come later, when Moresby could divulge that knowledge, gleaned presumably from Mr. Wargrave's colleagues. The object of the present interview had already been achieved, to see how Wargrave took the news that the identity of the dead girl, which her murderer had taken such precautions to keep hidden, was a mystery no longer.

And Moresby could not but admit to himself, as he put his routine questions and listened to Wargrave's ready but quite non-committal answers, that the shock of surprise had gained him precisely nothing at all.

On the other hand it was only natural to suppose that ever since the discovery of the body the murderer must have been keyed up to withstand just that shock, and certainly he had had plenty of time to rehearse his attitude.

CHAPTER X

WITH WARGRAVE DISMISSED THERE WAS NO LONGER any real need to keep the affair secret. When Moresby was invited, therefore, by a rather doubtful Miss Harrison who did not seem at all sure that he should not be relegated to the kitchen, to stay to lunch instead of looking for an inn in Allingford, he absolved from their oaths on this point those whom he had already interviewed.

These were Mr. Parker, Mr. Duff, and Mr. Rice. From none of them had he learnt anything at all, nor indeed had he expected to do so. All had been suitably shocked, all had appeared genuinely surprised that Miss Waterhouse of all people should have left the path of rectitude, all of them seemed to have been taken in by her just as much as the Harrisons had been, and not one of them breathed a word about any friendship between her and Wargrave. This was all no more nor less than Moresby had anticipated. It was from the women of the establishment that he hoped to learn something, if anything was to be learned at all; and by lifting the ban of silence and so loosening their tongues among themselves, he thought that something might be thrown up to the surface in their simmering chatter.

After lunch Leila Jevons was sent for.

Moresby took pains to put her at her ease. From the estimate he had formed of her from Roger Sheringham's manuscript, he considered her the most hopeful of all. She had known the dead girl as intimately as anyone had, she was a bit of a gossip, and she was of that eager type which is so very anxious to assist authority.

Moresby noticed with amused interest, as Miss Harrison introduced her, that there was no super-mole on the side of Miss Jevons's nose, nor yet any sign of one having existed. Evidently the great decision had been taken at last, with most satisfactory results.

Miss Jevons was at first inclined to flutter and bridle a little, but soon settled down under Moresby's practised handling. She leaned forward in her chair, her silken knees in plain evidence below her extremely short skirt, and looked almost painfully anxious to help. The turned-up tip of her mole-less nose shone and quivered.

"Yes?" she said. "Yes?"

"You knew Miss Waterhouse well, Miss Jevons?"

"Well, I—I thought I did. As well as anyone, you know. But she was always—well, what you might call close."

"She didn't talk as much as some girls?"

"Oh, no."

"Was she in the habit of confiding in you at all?"

"I don't think she was. I don't think she confided in anyone. She used to sit there, in my room, listening; and smiling, you know, but… Of course, she spoke about the Australian she was engaged to, but I expect you know all about him."

"Tell me as if I knew nothing at all, Miss Jevons, will you?"

Miss Jevons would, willingly; but it did not amount to very much. Mary had always spoken of him as "Ronald." Miss Jevons could not remember ever having heard his surname. Miss Jevons did not think she had ever heard an address mentioned; she had gathered that he had something to do with sheep-farming, but Miss Waterhouse had gone into no details. She had displayed a photograph of him, a small and exceedingly bad snapshot taken against a non-committal background, but really, it might have been anyone. No, Miss Jevons did not know what had become of the snapshot; presumably Miss Waterhouse had taken it with her at the end of term. Yes, she had said good-bye quite affectionately, but had still given no address; she had said she would write, from Australia; Miss Jevons had been quite hurt not to have heard.

"I see," nodded Moresby. He had never believed very much in the existence of this Australian, but that had not meant that he would not follow up every possible avenue of enquiry concerning him. He believed still less now.

"Now what," he asked next, "was the last you saw of Miss Waterhouse at the end of last summer term, Miss Jevons? Did you by any chance spend the first few days of the holidays together?"

No, Miss Jevons had not done that. The last she had seen of Miss Waterhouse was at Euston, whither the two had travelled up together, Miss Jevons to go to her home in Hampshire, and Miss Waterhouse, as she said, to meet her impatient Australian for lunch. Had Miss Waterhouse seemed quite normal at parting? Yes, quite. Not excited? Oh, no; Mary was never excited. Even though she was going to meet this rampant Australian? No, not even so.

Moresby pressed the point, and Miss Jevons readily agreed that she had been struck at the time by the singular calmness of Mary's demeanour; it had not been at all the expectant attitude of a girl about to greet an Australian lover. As Miss Jevons however gave Moresby the impression of being only too ready to agree with anything he suggested, he did not attach too much importance to her assent. Nevertheless it was a point.

"And now, Miss Jevons," he said, "I'm afraid I must venture on rather delicate ground. You know, I expect, that Miss Waterhouse was about to become a mother. Can you give me any suggestion as to who could possibly have been the father of her child?"

Miss Jevons was quite modern enough not to shrink from trying to help on this vital point, as Moresby had half-feared she might. "No, I'm afraid I can't," she said frankly. "I've been wondering that ever since I heard the girl at Lewisham was Mary. I can't imagine who the father could have been."

"Nobody here, for instance?"

"Oh, no, I don't think so, surely."

"Please try to think, Miss Jevons. You can understand the importance of it, I'm sure. Please see if you can't remember anything which would point to there having been something between Miss Waterhouse and somebody in Allingford—in this school. Have you never heard her mentioned in connection with any man?"

"Well, we used to rag her at one time about Mr. Wargrave,"

responded Miss Jevons promptly and obligingly, "but of course there was never anything like *that* between them. Besides, he's engaged to Miss Harrison now. They're going to be married next holidays."

"Yes. You don't know of any other man in connection with Miss Waterhouse then? She was never teased about anyone else?"

"No. The Australian was the only serious affair she had, I'm sure. He must be the father."

"I see. Thank you."

"Oo!" Miss Jevons's eyes grew round. "Does that mean it was he who…?"

"Come, come," said Moresby genially, "it's early to ask questions like that, you know; and earlier still for me to answer 'em." And having extracted all the information from Miss Jevons that she contained, he got benevolently rid of her.

Miss Crimp followed her into the morning-room, agog with anticipation.

Moresby, taking her measure with a practised eye, offered her a cigarette and adopted a firm air as of one who would stand no nonsense from any woman.

Miss Crimp however was not such a fool as Moresby had thought. Her judgement of Miss Waterhouse was shrewd.

"No, I never liked her much. And certainly I would never have trusted her. Oh, I don't mind a girl who doesn't smoke and doesn't drink and doesn't gossip. In fact they're rather refreshing nowadays, when they're genuine. But Mary Waterhouse wasn't genuine. I've seen her looking at my cigarette as if she could eat it. And all that clap-trap about duty and playing the game and the rest; she overdid it; it was nauseating. I tell you what. She gave me the impression always that she was playing a part of some kind—and having a bit of trouble in keeping it up. Of course, I may be prejudiced, because I did find all that smug talk of hers pretty sick-making; but I rather think I'm right for all that."

Moresby, reflecting that Miss Crimp knew nothing of Miss Mary Waterhouse's unexpected past, considered that this judgement did her powers of intuition no little credit. In her own way Miss Crimp might be just as much of a *poseuse* as Miss Waterhouse had been, but there was just as much real character underneath the pose.

"I didn't gather from the last young lady, Miss Jevons, that she thought that way about Miss Waterhouse," he remarked, with purposeful mildness.

"Oh, well," said Miss Crimp; and smiled. One was left to gather that Miss Jevons's powers of seeing beneath a surface were not high.

Moresby led her on, and by and by out plopped the name of Mr. Wargrave again. And Miss Crimp had a good deal more to say on this subject than Miss Jevons had had.

"Ah, yes," Moresby said carelessly. "But Miss Jevons assures me that there was nothing serious there."

"Oh, does she?" returned Miss Crimp darkly.

"You don't agree then? You think that Miss Waterhouse…?"

"I told you just now I wouldn't have trusted her an inch farther than I could see her."

"Yes. Now, Miss Crimp." Moresby's tone was portentous. "Now, Miss Crimp, an intelligent young lady like yourself will have realised that this is a very serious point. You're practically hinting that this Mr. Wargrave might have been the father of

Miss Waterhouse's child, aren't you? Now I want to ask you a very important question, and I must point out first that it is your duty to answer it as fully and as truthfully as you can; at the same time I'll add, a bit unofficially perhaps, that any answer you do give me will be treated as quite confidential between us and won't land you in any unpleasantness outside this room. Have you any kind of evidence at all, however small you yourself think it may be, in support of this hint of yours about Mr. Wargrave and Miss Waterhouse?"

"In other words, have I any evidence that Mr. Wargrave had a motive for murdering Mary?" said Miss Crimp acutely. "No, I haven't. If I had I'd tell you; because though I don't draw the line at much, I do draw it at murder. But evidence, no."

"You're certain of that?" Moresby said disappointedly.

"Quite. I only mentioned it because I think there's a distinct possibility of it, and I thought you ought to know. But I can only state the psychological case; not a practical one."

"Well, what evidence was there that there was anything at all between those two, even if it was only a mild flirtation?"

There was, it seemed, nothing more than the usual evidence in such cases. Mr. Wargrave and Miss Waterhouse had evidently been mildly attracted, had shown signs of liking each other's company, had made one or two expeditions to theatres in London, had been seen looking at each other like two people do who share a rather pleasant little secret; and of course Miss Waterhouse had been at one time in the habit of bridling slightly when teased about Mr. Wargrave. Nothing more.

Moresby nodded. He had already decided that this was the crux of his case. If he could prove Mr. Wargrave's paternity of the dead girl's child, he had such a strong motive against him that his guilt might be considered certain; and in that case the other details, connected with the actual killing, might with any luck be proved against him too. Without such proof, there was no basis to a case against Mr. Wargrave. That is, not at present. Of course, one never knows, in detective work. It would not be in the least out of the common for someone to crop up any day with the information that he had seen the couple actually going into the house in Burnt Oak Road together, and readily able to identify Wargrave as the man. It is that kind of thing, officially known as "information received," which brings to the gallows most of the murderers who are hanged.

One thing, however, Miss Crimp was able to establish. The interest shown by Miss Waterhouse and Mr. Wargrave in each other was not confined to the early part of the summer term, as Moresby had rather gathered, but had been in full swing during the previous Easter one. This was important.

Miss Crimp was dismissed with hearty words of praise and gratitude, and Mrs. Harrison followed her into the chamber of inquisition.

Phyllis Harrison, in a simple little black frock with a white collar, looked very innocent and disarming. Moresby was glad to have had Roger's side-lights on her.

Armed with these, Moresby went straight to the point.

"Madam," he said, without a trace of his usual geniality, "I have evidence that the father of Miss Waterhouse's unborn child was someone in this establishment. It is essential for me to find out who this man was, and I think you can help me."

The rather mocking smile which had been decorating Mrs. Harrison's pretty face disappeared abruptly. "You mean… that's why she was killed?"

"I couldn't go as far as to say that. On the other hand, the possibility must be examined."

"But—but it isn't a possibility, Chief Inspector. I mean, surely… Well, no one here could have done such a thing. It's impossible."

"On the contrary, madam," Moresby returned grimly, "it's extremely probable. You must face that, please. Now, you have certain resident masters here. Let me run through their names. Mr. Parker, Mr. Duff, Mr. Wargrave, Mr. Patterson, and Mr. Rice. As my information goes, one of those is the man I mean."

Mrs. Harrison was about to throw in an impetuous word, but Moresby raised an enormous hand to stop her.

"One moment, madam. I want to make this quite clear. I'm not accusing this man at the moment of being concerned in Miss Waterhouse's death. Nothing like that. On the other hand it's impossible to deny that her condition *may* have provided a motive. But that will come later. When you've confirmed my ideas on the point, we shall put the suspicion against him quite fairly and frankly to this man, and ask him for his explanation. It's quite possible that he will be able to satisfy us entirely; in which case we shall of course look elsewhere. But in the meantime (and I must emphasise this) it is your duty to help me by giving me all the information on this particular point that you have."

"But I haven't any," Phyllis retorted, a little sulkily.

"Mr. Parker, Mr. Duff, Mr. Wargrave, Mr. Patterson, and Mr. Rice," Moresby went on smoothly. "Now of those five I think we can eliminate straight away Mr. Rice." He looked at her fixedly.

"Y-yes?" Phyllis quavered, flinching under the meaning look.

Roger would not have recognised his benevolent walrus of a friend in the hard-eyed, hard-mouthed man who was staring at unfortunate little Mrs. Harrison. If Moresby got most of his results by exploiting his natural kindness of disposition, he knew exactly when to turn it into severity. Every weapon at his disposal must be used by a police officer in search of the truth.

"At the period in question," he said slowly, his eyes relentlessly boring into his victim's mind, "Mr. Rice's interests were, of course—how shall I put it, madam?—otherwise engaged. And I take it he is not the sort of man to have been carrying on two affairs at the same time. You agree with me?"

"Yes," whispered Mrs. Harrison.

There was a little silence, full of unspoken things.

"What is it you—want to know?" Mrs. Harrison asked, not very steadily.

"I told you. Any evidence you have that one of those three gentlemen had been carrying on an intrigue with Miss Waterhouse. You do know, don't you?"

"Yes," said Mrs. Harrison, in a husky voice.

"What do you know? The whole truth, please, madam."

"Last Easter term my step-daughter told me that she fancied there might be something—irregular going on, on the floor above us—at night," said Mrs. Harrison jerkily. "I heard someone moving along the upstairs passage one night, when I was going up to bed rather late. I—I went upstairs to see, and—and saw Miss Waterhouse, in her dressing-gown, just going into someone's room." Mrs. Harrison touched her lips with her handkerchief and looked at Moresby with frightened eyes.

"A man's?"

"Yes."

"Whose?"

"Mr. Wargrave's."

CHAPTER XI

MORESBY RETURNED TO SCOTLAND YARD FROM Allingford very pleased with himself. He had not expected to be able to obtain such definite evidence of the connection between Wargrave and the dead girl. Rumours he had anticipated, gossip, and scandal; but no real evidence. It was his feeling, as he made for the room of Superintendent Green to report, that Mrs. Harrison had put the rope round Wargrave's neck.

As was his habit, however, the superintendent was not so hopeful.

"Um!" he grunted, when Moresby had jubilantly told his news. "You've got motive all right, considering his engagement to the Harrison girl; but that's not much. We can't get a conviction on motive. By the way, I suppose the woman will be prepared to make that statement on oath?"

"Oh, yes," Moresby said, with a touch of grimness. In accordance with the tacit bargain he had made with Phyllis Harrison he had not mentioned even to the superintendent the lever by which he had been enabled to pry this information out of her. "Oh, yes, I don't think we'll have any difficulty there."

"But you've nothing corroborative? The maids were no use?"

After he had let Mrs. Harrison go, Moresby had proceeded with his interviewing of the rest of the staff, of the parlour-maid, Lily, and of the housemaid who looked after the rooms of the resident staff; but from none of them had he been able to obtain either corroboration of Mrs. Harrison's testimony or any fresh information. Privately he did not consider that this mattered, but he knew that the superintendent would not see eye to eye with him on that point. Superintendent Green held the theory that no piece of evidence was really worth anything unless there was definite corroboration of it, a theory which, Moresby considered, had given its holder a good deal of unnecessary bother in working up his cases.

"No, sir," he said now. "I've no corroboration." He did not add that in his opinion no corroboration was needed. "But there's all the gossip about the two of them. That's almost as good."

"Um," observed Superintendent Green, implying that it wasn't. "Well, what do you propose to do next?"

"I thought of getting this Wargrave up here, and asking if he'd like to say anything about it."

"Make a statement, eh?"

"Yes."

"And account for his movements after the end of term?"

"Well, I should like to hear what you think about that, Mr. Green. It's my opinion that if I ask him that now he'll go mum and refuse to say a word without a solicitor. He strikes me as that sort. And then it would only give away the fact that he's under suspicion, and we'd get nothing out of it."

"Whereas…?"

"Why, if I only have a friendly chat with him about the girl, as you might say, there's no call for him to think anything else, is there? And if he did let drop something, well, we could follow it up a bit before we asked him about his movements."

His superior officer eyed Moresby with some distaste. A blunt man himself, Superintendent Green preferred blunt methods. "Trying to be a bit tricky, aren't you?"

"He's a tricky one himself, sir," deprecated Moresby.

"Then he'll see through you. No, you can do which you like, Moresby, but in your place I'd go straight for his movements. After all, it's going to take us some time to check up on them after all these months, and it's my opinion that the sooner you get on to that the better."

"Very well, Mr. Green," Moresby agreed, with concealed resignation. "In that case I'd better go through everything with him. What he knows about building, I mean, and all that."

"I should say so. Take a full statement from him. And if he wants a solicitor, of course he must have one."

"Of course." It was obvious that Moresby considered solicitors in the light of an obstacle in the paths of justice. Perhaps Moresby was not very wrong.

Superintendent Green began to stuff an ancient briar pipe. "Well, what do you propose to do about the other end? Assuming you get nothing out of this Wargrave, where are you then? You know as well as I do that you'll never get a conviction unless you can prove a connection between him and that house in Lewisham. How are you going to do that?"

"I got hold of a snapshot of the girl at the school. It's not a very good one, but there was no portrait. I've sent it up to the photographer to have an enlargement made, and as soon as I've got that Fox can take it down to Lewisham and find out if the neighbours recognise it."

"That's all right. And what about him?"

"There'll be a photo of him going down to Lewisham with Fox too," said Moresby, with as near an approach to a wink as a chief inspector may well bestow on a superintendent.

"How did you get that?"

"I met Blair, of the *Evening Star*, just outside when I was leaving. I told him that if he could get photographs for me of the staff, I might have something for him when the time's ripe."

"Um." Superintendent Green expressed neither approval nor the reverse of this Machiavellian manoeuvre. He lit his pipe, and puffed at it for a moment in silence.

"Of course," he said, after the pause, "as I said three or four months ago, the case would be clear enough as soon as the girl was identified. But it's going to be a dickens of a case to prove. I know that, as well as you do. In fact, if the man used just ordinary precautions in getting her into the house (and I'll bet he did that), and if nothing crops up to connect him with the house or Miss Staples in any other way—well, it's going to be about as difficult a job as you've tackled yet, young Moresby."

"It is that, Mr. Green," assented young Moresby gloomily, as he rose to go. "But we'll get him yet, somehow." His words expressed a good deal more optimism than he felt. It is an irritating position, but one in which Scotland Yard not infrequently finds itself, to know perfectly well who committed a particular crime and yet be unable to make the arrest for lack of proof sufficient to convince a jury. And in this case there was as yet hardly any proof at all.

Moresby went back to his small bachelor flat to spend an evening in racking his brains; and the process did neither him nor the case any good at all.

The first job next morning was to send Inspector Fox off to Lewisham, with the enlarged snapshot of Miss Waterhouse and the photograph of Wargrave from among those sent along by the reporter of the *Evening Star*. Moresby had little hope of any results from the visitation.

In the meantime Sergeant Afford had gone off to Allingford in a police car to ask Mr. Wargrave, very politely, whether he would be good enough to accompany him back to Scotland Yard, as Chief Inspector Moresby wished to ask him a few further questions arising out of their interview yesterday. Mr. Wargrave was not informed that an unobtrusive person who had travelled down with the sergeant to Allingford had slipped out of the car at the entrance to the drive, taken cover behind some bushes until the car had passed him on its return journey with Mr. Wargrave unmistakably in the back seat, and then gone up to Roland House to present a search-warrant with the request that he might be turned loose in the room lately occupied by Miss Waterhouse. And even if he had been so informed, he might not have understood that the unobtrusive one's real object, as soon as he was left alone upstairs in Roland House, was not the room lately occupied by Miss Waterhouse, but the room occupied at present by Mr. Wargrave.

As a matter of principle Moresby kept Wargrave waiting for twenty minutes or so before sending for him. He had found that the atmosphere of Scotland Yard, allowed thus to sink slowly into anyone with a guilty conscience, tends to produce considerable pain and confusion in the mind of the suspect.

No signs of pain or confusion were present, however, in Mr. Wargrave's completely impassive face as he took the chair into which Moresby pressed him. He did not look even annoyed, as Moresby noticed with interest, in spite of his twenty minutes' wait. In such cases, while the guilty are hard put to it to conceal a certain trepidation, the innocent are often angry and show it.

At a table in a corner of the room sat a detective-constable with a knowledge of shorthand, and a paper-pad in front of him. Wargrave had not so much as glanced at him.

A cool customer, thought Moresby, not without admiration, as he sat down and faced the other across his desk.

"Now, sir," he began, briskly enough, "I'm sorry I had to bring you here, but there are a few things I want to discuss with you that I thought we could go into better here than at Roland House."

Wargrave nodded shortly. So far he had not spoken a word beyond "Good morning."

"They're mostly concerned with your relations with Miss Waterhouse. I thought perhaps you might like to make a statement concerning them."

Wargrave raised his heavy black eyebrows. "A statement?" he repeated, almost indifferently. "What on earth is there to make a statement about?"

"As I said, Mr. Wargrave, your relations with Miss

Waterhouse. You need not of course make a statement if you don't wish to do so. I have no power to compel you, not even to answer my questions; and it is my duty to warn you that anything you do say is entirely at your own risk."

"Very kind of you, indeed," said Wargrave drily. "But I'm afraid I don't understand. I had no 'relations' with Miss Waterhouse."

Moresby changed his tone to a less official one. "Now see here, sir, I don't want you to think that I'm bluffing you, or trying to make you incriminate yourself by a trick, or anything like that. We don't do that sort of thing here. So I'll lay my cards on the table, and you can play to them or not just as you like. You know Miss Waterhouse was going to have a baby. I have certain evidence that you might have been its father. And, frankly, I should like to hear what you have to say on the matter."

"Then I'll tell you at once," returned Wargrave, not in the least perturbed. "Nothing!—Evidence, indeed. A lot of silly feminine gossip."

Moresby looked at him. "Oh, no, Mr. Wargrave. Something much more serious than that. When I say evidence, I mean evidence. I've no objection to telling you what it is. Miss Waterhouse was seen one night, nearly a year ago, going into your room."

The shot had got home. There was no doubt about that. For just a fraction of a second a flicker passed across the man's face. The next instant he had recovered.

"Nonsense. Who says so?"

"I'm afraid I can't tell you that."

"I thought not," Wargrave sneered.

"Oh, I'm not inventing it, sir, if that's what you mean. Am I to understand then that you deny anything of the kind?"

"Certainly I do. If anyone did tell you such a preposterous thing, it's a blank lie. That's all."

"But relations of that kind did exist between you and Miss Waterhouse."

"You'll pardon me, they did not. Nothing of the sort."

"You deny them completely?"

"Completely."

Moresby sighed. He had known Wargrave was going to be difficult, and he was being difficult.

"Very well, Mr. Wargrave. But if I were to suggest to you that Miss Waterhouse herself had confided to a friend…?"

"I should call you an infernal liar," retorted Wargrave promptly.

Moresby, who knew only too well that that is exactly what he would be did he make any such suggestion, sighed again.

He tried a fresh cast. "You were in the war, sir?"

"I was."

"You don't mind telling me which regiment?"

"Not in the least. The Northamptons."

"You saw active service with them?"

"I did. The Seventh Service Battalion."

"You had a revolver, of course?"

"Of course."

"A service revolver, or an automatic?"

"An ordinary service revolver."

"Have you got it still?"

This time Moresby was not so certain, but he fancied that the little flicker had again passed across Wargrave's face. There was, however, no perceptible hesitation before he answered:

"No."

"How is that?"

"Do you mean, what has happened to it? I never brought it back to England at all. I was wounded in 1918, July, and my revolver was lost, with most of my kit."

"I see. Then you haven't had it in your possession at all since the war?"

"That was what I was trying to convey."

"Have you had any other revolver in your possession at any time since the war?"

"No."

A blank end again. But at any rate Wargrave had not demanded the presence of a solicitor before he answered any questions. In a way Moresby rather wished that he had. The demand for a solicitor means the fear of incriminating oneself; and that usually means guilt. Wargrave seemed to be contemptuously dismissing the possibility of incriminating himself. The man's self-confidence was enormous. And so far, Moresby had to admit, quite justified.

He dropped his eyes from the ceiling, where they had been resting since Wargrave's final denial of the possession of any shape, kind, or semblance of a revolver, and fastened them once more on the other's face.

"Mr. Wargrave, have you any objection to making a statement as to your movements immediately after the end of your last summer term?"

"Not the least," Wargrave replied calmly, "if I can remember them. But I really would like to get this straight first.

Have you or have you not got me under suspicion of having murdered Miss Waterhouse?" And he gave the chief inspector a short, humourless smile.

For perhaps the first time in his official life Moresby found himself somewhat taken aback. It was the use of the word "murder" that had effected this phenomenon. Murderers never "murder." Whoever else may murder, they do not. They may "slay": they sometimes even "kill": but they never, never "murder." Moresby knew that the use of the word was bluff, but it was a kind of bluff to which he was unaccustomed. His opinion that Wargrave was a cool customer was confirmed.

He did not answer the question directly. "It's part of our routine here, sir, that everyone who was in contact with a murdered person shortly before the crime, should give an account of his or her movements at the time. There's no question of suspicion in my asking you to do so. I shall take a dozen similar statements in connection with the death of Miss Waterhouse."

"I quite understand," said Wargrave, and smiled again. Moresby had no difficulty in interpreting the smile. It said to him, quite plainly: Yes, you know I did it, and I know I did it, but you'll never, never prove it, my good man.

"Well, then, Mr. Wargrave," he said, and added to the constable: "Gravestock, take this down, please."

Wargrave assumed an expression of deep thought. "Last summer term, now. Let me see. So far as I remember I left Allingford by the 11.17, to Euston, as usual. From there I took a taxi with my luggage to Charing Cross, and left my bags in the cloak-room. I forget how I spent the afternoon; doing odd jobs and so on; I think I turned into a cinema for a time.

Anyhow, I caught a train at about six o'clock from Charing Cross to Grove Park, in Kent, where I was going to stay a week with a friend of mine. Wait a minute—was it those holidays? Yes, that's right; I'm sure it was."

"The name of your friend, sir?"

"Duffield. John Duffield. Wife's name, Margaret Duffield. He's employed at the British Museum. I was staying there just over a week. I can't give you the exact dates. They may be able to."

"Had you any particular reason for staying there?"

"I don't understand you. Does one have to have a particular reason for staying with a friend? As a matter of fact I did invite myself, now you remind me. And yes, I had a particular reason. I had been giving some lectures at Roland House the previous term on elementary science, a subject in which I am interested, and I'd found that my knowledge on certain points had got very rusty. I wanted to put in a few days at the Science Museum, in South Kensington. I couldn't afford to stay at an hotel in London, and I therefore asked Mr. Duffield if he could put me up. I had a standing invitation to go there whenever I wished; Mr. Duffield is a very old friend of mine."

Moresby nodded. Wargrave had an explanation for everything, of course.

"Yes, and then?"

"Then I went home. Twenty-seven Alma Road, Clitheroe, Lancashire, is my parents' address. I stayed there for the rest of the holidays."

"And the date on which you went to Clitheroe?"

"I can't possibly tell you."

"And you visited the Science Museum while you were staying at Grove Park?"

"Certainly. I spent a lot of time there."

"Every day?"

"No. Most days."

"Can you tell me which days you spent there, and approximately how much time on each day?"

"I can't. I don't keep a diary."

"You can't give me any idea at all?"

"None, I'm afraid."

"I see. Now, Mr. Wargrave, I'm going to ask you a question which there's no need for you to answer if you don't care to do so. Did you on any of those days on which you came up to London from Grove Park, or at any other time during your stay at Grove Park, see Miss Waterhouse?"

"I've no objection at all to answering. I did not."

"Thank you, sir."

"That all I can do for you?" Wargrave asked ironically.

"That's all, Mr. Wargrave. If you'll just go back to the waiting-room while your statement is being typed out, I'll ask you to read it through and, if you approve of it, sign it; and after that, of course, you'll be quite free to go."

Wargrave smiled without speaking.

Moresby summoned a constable to conduct him back to the waiting-room.

As soon as he had gone, the chief inspector lifted the telephone receiver and put through a call to Clitheroe police station. In the interval of waiting he called up the station at Grove Park, and gave certain instructions.

Then, having arranged for Wargrave to be shadowed when

he left the building, Chief Inspector Moresby leaned back in his chair and frowned heavily at his desk.

As he had expected, the interview had left him almost exactly where he had been before.

"Well, he *is* a cool one all right," said Chief Inspector Moresby handsomely.

CHAPTER XII

"Afford, my lad," said Moresby after lunch. "I've got a rotten job for you. Take this photograph of Wargrave to Euston"—the excellent Blair had provided duplicates of all his photographs—"see if you can get hold of the porter who handled his luggage on the 2nd April last year, and find out if one of his cases was exceptionally heavy. Then go on to Charing Cross and do the same there. He put his luggage in the cloak-room at Charing Cross, so there'll be two porters and a cloak-room man who handled it there. And if you can find any of 'em I'll stand you a glass of beer this evening with my own hands."

Afford grinned. "I'm afraid I'll go dry, then. It's the cement?"

"It's the cement," Moresby nodded. "You remember, there was none *under* the bricks, only between the joints. He could have carried enough for that job, ready mixed with the sand, in a suit-case. The proportion was two to one if that will help you, but it won't. In any event, it was a tidy weight."

"He wouldn't have taken it down to Grove Park though, would he? If he had his plans all cut and dried, he probably took that particular case along to Lewisham at once, supposing he had it with him at all."

"One of the 'odd jobs' he says he was doing that afternoon. Yes, I know all about that. Probably he didn't have it with him at all. Probably he'd either taken it up before, or went back to Allingford for it afterwards. As soon as Fox has finished at Lewisham he's going down to Allingford to find out whether Wargrave was seen near the place after the term was over. In the meantime, you see what you can do. But bless us," added Moresby with a sigh, "I've a feeling we're not going to connect that cement with him. He's been too cunning, and that's a fact. Send Johnson up as you go out, Afford."

Johnson was the unobtrusive person who had presented the search-warrant at Roland House that morning.

His report, negative for the most part, contained one interesting suggestion.

"Nothing at all, Mr. Moresby," he said. "No letters, no photograph of her, nothing to connect 'em whatever. But I'll take my oath he had a revolver."

"'*Had?*'" repeated Moresby sharply.

"Had. At the back of the bottom drawer in his chest-of-drawers there was a wodge of old cotton-wool with a deep impression in the middle of it. I took the measurements, and if it wasn't a service revolver that made it I'll be very surprised. There was a smear or two of oil on the wool too. But there's no revolver in his room now."

Moresby said a bad word. "He's got rid of it since yesterday, that's what he's done. Hell's bells, I ought to have had the place watched. It's my fault. But it's pretty smart work on his part. Still, I ought to have allowed for it. Goodness knows I knew he was smart enough. Johnson, get back to Allingford at once, *and find that revolver.* Understand? Don't you come back here without it. Find out his movements after I left yesterday afternoon, imagine what he'd have done if he went out at night, search everywhere there is to search. And when you've found it, get hold of a witness before you remove it. Then bring it back to me here. Off with you."

Johnson went, with a rueful grin.

Moresby was annoyed with himself. He should have put a watch on Wargrave yesterday. He had made the bad mistake of underestimating the other's resourcefulness. Moresby did not care to think what Superintendent Green would have to say about such a lapse.

He pulled the dossier of the case towards him and began flicking over the pages, before fastening in a copy of the enlargement of the snapshot of Mary Waterhouse, sent down from the photographic department that morning. An idea occurred to him. He drew the house-telephone towards him, and asked for the department in question.

"That you, Merriman? Remember that snapshot I sent up to you yesterday for enlargement? Yes, the Waterhouse case. No, it hasn't come out too badly at all. Yes, quite recognisable, I should say. Well, I want a lot more copies. What? Yes, for the papers. Oh, say three dozen. Can you push 'em through this afternoon? Thanks. Oh, and I'm sending up another photograph. Name of Wargrave. Yes, same case. Better let me have a dozen of him. Yes. Thanks."

He took a piece of paper and began to draft out a note to the Press, asking them to display the portrait of Miss Waterhouse with a discreetly worded caption to the effect that the police would be glad of information from anyone who had seen her alive at any time during the previous August.

For here was one of the blank periods of the case. From the moment Leila Jevons said good-bye to her at Euston, Miss Waterhouse seemed to have vanished utterly. The moment he got back from Allingford on the previous afternoon Moresby had put two of his best men on to tracing her and finding out where she had spent that first week of August, but so far they had had no luck. It was true that they had not yet been twenty-four hours on the job, but twenty-four hours should have been ample to unearth the taxi that had driven her from Euston if it was ever to be found at all. Evidently it was not. The interval was too great for any driver to remember what had no doubt been a perfectly ordinary journey. But the gap was a bad one.

Having completed the chit, Moresby pushed the dossier away from him and betook himself to some of the other work which had been piling up for the last forty-eight hours.

Shortly before six o'clock Inspector Fox returned. He had had a blank day. Not a single one of the neighbours, nor the vicar, nor the house-agent, nor even the local Mabels had recognised either of the photographs.

"Hell!" said Moresby simply.

"It's a brute of a case, sir," ventured Inspector Fox.

Moresby frowned at him morosely.

"Then how the hell did one of them get hold of the key to the house? That's what I want to know. It's no use telling me they might not have had a key. They *must* have had one, to have got in without leaving any traces like that."

"And apart from that, how did they know the house was going to be empty like that? You'd say that one of them must have been in touch with either Miss Staples or the neighbours."

"I would, and I do," Moresby snapped. "After all, failure to recognise a photo isn't conclusive. Slip a pair of horn spectacles on, and people like that'll swear they've never seen you before."

"I might get a pair of horn spectacles drawn on those photos and try again, Mr. Moresby."

"Oh, don't take me so damned literally, man!"

Inspector Fox, who had only been trying to be helpful, retired hurt, and Moresby continued to gloom at him.

"There's one way she might have got hold of that key," he said slowly, after a considerable pause.

"Sir?" said Inspector Fox, in the unenthusiastic tones of one unjustly snapped at.

"She was a bag-thief, wasn't she? Suppose she once stole Miss Staples's bag, and it had her address inside, and her key. That would account for the key, wouldn't it?"

"That's right enough, Mr. Moresby," generously agreed Inspector Fox. "It would."

Moresby had taken up the telephone as he spoke, and now asked for the Lewisham police station, and then for the sergeant in charge.

"This is Chief Detective Inspector Moresby speaking, Sergeant. You remember that murder in Burnt Oak Road. I want you to look up your records at once and tell me whether you ever had a complaint from Miss Staples, at No. 4, that her bag had been stolen, or her purse, or anything of that nature. Within the last few years. I'll hold on."

Moresby did not have to wait long. The invaluable card-index produced the information at once. Miss Staples had had her bag stolen, just over three years ago, in a bus in the Old Kent Road. There had been little of value in it, a few shillings, her latch-key, a handkerchief marked "M.S." There was no record that the bag had ever been recovered.

"Well, that clears up one difficulty," Moresby remarked, not without satisfaction, as he hung up the receiver. "It's a hundred pounds to a farthing that it was Miss Mary Weller, as she was then, who got that bag. And she kept the key by her all that time, just for luck. Well, it's nice to know it; but I don't see that it's going to help us much for all that."

"And it doesn't explain how they knew about the neighbours."

"No," Moresby said thoughtfully, his good temper quite recovered now. "And I've a sort of an idea that it would help us a good deal to find that out. But I'm blessed if I can see how we're going to do it at the moment."

He scratched his head for a few moments over the problem, gave it up, and looked at his notes.

"Here's your job to-morrow, Fox. I've found that the girl used to wear an engagement ring. One she said had been given her by the Australian. It was a good ring, they tell me; here's as close a description of it as I could get—three diamonds with two emeralds set between 'em, in platinum. It's all down here. Find out if any ring answering that description has been sold or offered for sale in London since the first of August last year."

Fox nodded. It was an arduous job, but one to which he was well accustomed.

"You'll probably have no luck," Moresby added, as he rose. "On the other hand Wargrave strikes me as a man who wouldn't throw a good ring away, even if it did come to him through a bit of nasty work." On this cynical note, Moresby struggled into his overcoat and picked up his hat.

"You think she had it on when they went to the house?" asked Fox, as they walked down the echoing stone passage.

"I *know* she had it on, my lad," corrected Moresby, who knew nothing of the sort. "And why? Because it's the only possible explanation for those gloves she was wearing. I told the super that weeks ago. Mr. Smartie thought that if we saw a girl with gloves on and no rings under 'em, we'd go about looking for a girl without any rings. But Mr. Smartie forgot that a nice diamond ring will make a nice mark on the inside of a glove; and there the mark was, sure enough. Reminds me of a fellow who writes detective stories, Mr. Smartie does: too smart by half."

Inspector Fox laughed heartily.

Moresby was not going back to his own flat. He had rung up Roger Sheringham earlier in the afternoon to ask if he might call in on his way home to ask a question or two about Roger's friend at Roland House, who had of course not figured in the manuscript; and Roger had bade him to dinner. Moresby, knowing what Roger's dinners were, had accepted. Secretly too, though he would have died rather than admit as much to Mr. Sheringham, who was quite bumptious enough already, he wanted to talk over the case with him. An outside mind (as Moresby excused this weakness to himself) can sometimes disentangle threads that to one whose eye is nearer to them seem inextricably jumbled.

Roger welcomed his guest with smiles and an excellent dry sherry.

"Patterson?" he said, when they were seated before the fire, for this was the name of the pedagogic friend. "Oh, you can put him out of your mind. You saw him, I suppose?"

"I interviewed him one of the last, not knowing him from your book. He couldn't tell me anything of any use."

"No, I don't suppose he could, except how funny it would all have been if it hadn't been so tragic. Patterson's one of the few schoolmasters I've met who've preserved their sense of proportion. But in this affair he won't be any help to you."

"You've spoken to him yourself, Mr. Sheringham?" Moresby asked suspiciously.

Roger smiled. "I rang him up yesterday evening. You left them all very upset, Moresby."

"Did I?" Moresby said callously. "Well, well."

"Patterson didn't say much, but I gathered that opinion there seems to have crystallised."

"Meaning…?"

"That it coincides with your own," Roger said drily.

"In other words—Wargrave?"

"Yes."

Moresby absently examined his sherry against the light.

"And you, Mr. Sheringham? You agree too?"

"It's pretty beastly, but…what else can one think? Got a case against him?"

"Plenty. But no proof. It's like this."

Moresby ran through the difficulties of the case.

"Every line we follow seems to have a dead end," he concluded ruefully. "Except how she got hold of the key, of course; and that's of no real importance."

"What's this about her stealing a bag?"

"Oh, I forgot. You don't know about that. She was a bad lot, Mr. Sheringham." Moresby explained that too.

"By Jove!" Roger admired. "Well, she certainly carried it off well. She certainly took me in."

Moresby nobly refrained from mentioning that she had not taken in Miss Crimp.

"Blackmail, then?" Roger continued. "Powerful motive. She was trying to get in the way of his marrying Amy Harrison, of course. Yes, it's all quite clear. Poor girl, she'd got the wrong man. I wouldn't like to cross Wargrave myself. But I shouldn't have expected him to descend to murder, you know, Moresby. Murder's a sign of weakness when all's said and done, and Wargrave's a strong man. I should have expected him to take a firmer line."

"It seems difficult to find a firmer line than murder, Mr. Sheringham."

"Not a bit of it. There's far more courage needed to tell a blackmailer to go to hell than to kill him, or her. Far more. Still, that's beside the point, as he did take that line. So what are the police going to do about it?"

"We're doing a good deal about it, sir; but it doesn't seem to be carrying us far."

"No. In fact between ourselves, Moresby, I don't think you're going to get him. I don't see what more you could possibly do than you are doing; but you'll never convict him without a great deal more."

"No, Mr. Sheringham." Moresby fingered the stem of his glass with an absent air.

It was Roger's turn to be suspicious. "Moresby, what have you got in your mind? You didn't come here just to talk about Patterson. What is it?"

Moresby grinned. "I'll tell you, Mr. Sheringham. I want your help on this case, and that's the truth."

"My help?"

"Yes. You see, sir, it's like this. Roland House is a big place. It's impossible for one of our men to watch it properly. Except perhaps at night, he'd have to stop outside the grounds; and what's the good of that, in twenty or thirty acres?"

"Well?"

"Well, you've worked with us often enough before for me to get permission for you to do so again. I want someone inside Roland House. Could you arrange with your friend for him to go sick, and for you to take his place again?"

"You mean, you want me to be a spy within the gates, so to speak? To keep an eye on Wargrave, and at the same time ferret out what I can to incriminate him?"

"That's it, sir," said Moresby with enthusiasm. "That's just what I want."

"Well, I won't touch it. That's flat. Any other case, and with pleasure; but not among people I know. No, Moresby, an amateur detective may have few standards left, but I haven't come down to spying on my friends yet. I wouldn't think of it."

"That's a pity. You'd rather the murderer went free, then, sir?"

"Don't put the responsibility for his going free on me. You catch him. It's your job, not mine."

"Humph!" said Moresby. "I'm not asking you to catch him, Mr. Sheringham. I'm going to do that myself. All I want you to do is to see that he doesn't commit suicide, or go murdering somebody else, or destroy important evidence like that revolver. That's all."

Roger laughed. "It's no good. I won't go. I'll talk the case over with you as much as you like, but take an active hand in it I will not."

Moresby gloomed into his sherry, and was understood to mumble that a fat lot of good talking would do, it was evidence he wanted.

"One little bit of real evidence to connect that man with the murder, Mr. Sheringham. That's all I'm asking at present, just as a sweetener after two months' work. It's not much to want, is it? But I'm blessed if I can get it."

The small gods who lie in wait for that kind of remark were not asleep. It was precisely at that moment that Roger's telephone-bell rang.

"Yes?" he said. "Yes, he's here. Hold on, please. Moresby, someone wants you."

Moresby, who had left word at Scotland Yard where he could be found, jumped up and took the receiver.

"Is that Chief Inspector Moresby?"

"Speaking."

"Sergeant Johnson here, sir; speaking from Allingford. I thought you'd like to know at once: we've got the revolver."

"You have? Well done. Who's 'we'?"

"Me and Gregory, sir." It was Detective-Constable Gregory who had been detailed to tail Wargrave when he left Scotland Yard.

"How did you find it?" Moresby asked jubilantly.

"Well, sir, I connected up with Gregory when I got here. He told me the party came straight back here, so I told him to stay with me and we'd both work where we could keep a bit of an eye on the house. I'd brought a camera with me, meaning to say I was a newspaper-man if anyone wanted to know what I was doing, so I told Gregory to take it and be the camera-man and I'd be the reporter. I searched a lot of places some distance away from the house, but couldn't find anything, and meant to work nearer after dark. Consequently, me and Gregory were approaching the house at about dusk, when out comes the party.

"He had a good look round, but didn't see us, because I pulled Gregory behind a clump of rhododendrons as soon as I spotted him. Well, he set off at a smart walk, and we followed. He took us across the playing-field and began to walk down a hedge on the farther side, slowly, as if he was looking for a place. It was pretty dark, so me and Gregory worked round the hedge at right-angles to his hedge and were able to get fairly close to him. I thought I'd better take Gregory with me on account of what you said about a witness."

"Yes, yes," Moresby said impatiently.

"Well, after a bit he seemed to have come to the right place, and stooped down. I saw he was busy searching in the hedge, so me and Gregory closed in to within a few yards of him. When he stood up I took a chance that he'd got what he was looking for, and went up to him. He'd got the revolver in his hand. He threatened me with it, and I closed with him, while Gregory got the revolver away from him. I told Gregory to be careful of handling it."

"Good heavens, man, Gregory knows how to handle a revolver."

"I mean, because of the prints it might have on it, sir!" almost squeaked Sergeant Johnson, in extremely hurt tones.

"Oh, I see. Yes, well done, Johnson. Very thoughtful. Yes, and then?"

"Well, that's all, sir. I told him I must take charge of it, and I brought it away with me, wrapped in a handkerchief. Because of the prints," added Sergeant Johnson.

"And the party?"

"Well, sir, I did think of putting him under arrest for being in possession of fire-arms without a licence, and then I thought perhaps you mightn't want it, so I came here to telephone you for instructions. We saw the party back to the house, and then left together. Outside the gates I sent Gregory back with instructions to get into the grounds unobserved and watch the house, and, if the party went out, tail him. Would you like me to go back and put him under arrest, Mr. Moresby?"

"No," Moresby said, after a second's thought. "We really haven't enough to hold him on yet. Bring the revolver to headquarters at once, Johnson. You'll find me in my room. I shall want to see you before you go. You've done very well."

"Thank you, Mr. Moresby," said the gratified Johnson, and rang off.

Moresby hung up the receiver and came back to the fire beaming and rubbing his hands. "Well, thank you, sir," he said, as Roger silently handed him his refilled glass. "I don't mind if I do. Well, you heard that? We've got the revolver."

"So I gathered. Your one little bit of real evidence that you were bleating for a minute ago."

"That's right, sir, that's right. And now the luck's going to turn. You see if it doesn't."

"You'll need it," Roger said drily. "It isn't a capital offence to own a revolver, is it? And you've nothing to show that this is the revolver which committed the crime."

"No, no, that's true enough. We haven't got the bullet, you see. No, it doesn't connect him with the crime really, but the circumstances will look bad when they're put before a jury. Very bad. It would have been better for him if he'd left the thing innocently in his drawer. It's the first proper mistake he's made. Well, now he's begun making them, let's hope he goes on."

"It was a very foolish mistake," Roger agreed, rather wonderingly. It was not the kind of mistake he would have expected Wargrave to make. It was beginning to dawn on Roger that he must have read that beetle-browed man not altogether correctly.

"He got rid of the revolver from his bedroom yesterday after I'd gone, just in case," Moresby pronounced. "I don't suppose he thought he was really under suspicion then, but he wasn't taking any chances. Then this morning of course in my room he did know we had our eye on him, and he knew we'd be making search for the weapon sooner or later in the grounds of Roland House; so the sooner he got rid of it properly the better. I wonder what he was going to do with it. There is a canal somewhere near, isn't there? Yes, the Grand Junction runs through those parts. That's where he was probably going to pitch it. And he'd have got away with it too, if by a bit of luck I hadn't sent Johnson down to look for it." Moresby's tone implied, however, that luck was not really the right word, which only modesty forbade him to employ.

Roger eyed him with distaste. When there was any bragging of his own to do Roger had no hesitation in doing it; but he hated to have to listen to others. "Hurry up with your sherry, Moresby. Dinner's due."

"Dinner, Mr. Sheringham? I'm afraid I can't stay to dinner now. I've got to get back to headquarters, to meet Johnson."

"Good heavens, Johnson can wait. Meadows will never forgive you if you don't eat what he's got ready—nor me either, which is much more serious. Besides, it's *tripes à la mode de Caen*."

"It's what, sir?"

"Tripe."

"Tripe?"

"Tripe."

"Johnson," said Moresby, "can wait."

CHAPTER XIII

THE REVOLVER DID ALL THAT WAS EXPECTED OF IT, AND more. So much more that Roger, when he heard about it later, marvelled at the fatuity of one whom he had set down as an intelligent man.

In the first place it showed one man's finger-prints only. As Wargrave had been seen with it actually in his hand, it was indisputable that these were his, although there was no official set with which to compare them. In the second place it had not even been cleaned. The barrel was rusted and full of fouling, which the experts pronounced to be approximately six months old. And thirdly, it was loaded in five chambers, while in the sixth was an empty case.

Except for the all-important fact that there was nothing to establish that it was this particular revolver which had killed Mary Waterhouse, it might have been enough to have hanged Wargrave.

More than ever Moresby deplored the loss of the bullet. Now that the experts can decide whether a certain bullet was fired from a certain weapon or not, the bullet has become as important as the weapon. With the bullet in his possession Moresby could have arrested Wargrave and been practically certain of a conviction. Without it, except for the fact that Wargrave had behaved suspiciously, the case against him was scarcely advanced.

Moresby debated whether he should send for him to Scotland Yard again.

The episode warranted another interrogation, if anything could be gained by it. Besides the actual hiding of the revolver, too, there was the threatening with it of Johnson. Had Wargrave really meant to shoot Johnson? Johnson seemed to think so. But then Johnson, though a sound man, was inclined to think things that made for his own importance. It would be very foolish of Wargrave if he really had had any such intention. On the whole Moresby did not believe that he had. Johnson had probably mistaken a purely instinctive action of surprise for a threat.

Moresby decided not to send for Wargrave again just yet. He would wait until something else turned up on which the man could be interrogated as well. Wargrave would undoubtedly be expecting a summons, and would have his story all pat; when it did not come he would be wondering what was happening and why he had not been sent for. He would know that the revolver episode could not be left in abeyance. By all the rules he should become worried and anxious; and when a murderer becomes worried and anxious he usually does something foolish. Moresby hoped very much, but without a great deal of faith, that Wargrave would do something foolish.

A messenger interrupted his musings with a chit.

Moresby opened it. It was from the Records Office of the Army Ordnance Department, and was in answer to a query he had sent them first thing that morning.

"In reply to your telephone message, service revolver No. D. 7748 was issued on 14th September, 1917, to Second-Lieutenant Wargrave, 7th Batt., Northamptonshire Regiment."

The revolver had said all that it possibly could say, without its bullet.

It had said, too, all that was said in the case at all for the next day or two. The other tentacles which Moresby had put out came back empty. Sergeant Afford, having questioned all the porters, and the ex-porters too, at Euston and Charing Cross, and the cloak-room men, and the ticket-inspectors, and everyone else whom he could think of to question, had been unable to find the slightest trace of any extra-heavy suit-case passing through either of the stations eleven months ago. Inspector Fox had no more luck in tracing the ring. The two enquiries were written off as part of the usual loss of time and energy which a difficult case invariably entails.

Meanwhile a close watch was kept on Wargrave, which also was quite without result. He scarcely went outside the school grounds, and then only to buy tobacco in the village or for some equally harmless purpose. Enquiries of course had been unobtrusively in progress ever since the body had been identified, among the villagers and residents of Allingford; but except for the connecting links of Miss Crimp and the Rev. Michael Stanford, the two communities of Allingford and Roland House had scarcely any ties; in any case the enquiries had brought nothing to fruition, not even the usual crop of rumours which might have been expected had Roland House not been so self-contained and cut off from the rest of Allingford.

It seemed as if the case was dead.

On the third day after the finding of the revolver it sprang once more into vivid life.

The news editor of the *Daily Courier* rang up Scotland Yard, and the call was switched through to Moresby's room.

"You remember that photograph of the Waterhouse girl you sent us, Chief Inspector?" he said. "Well, I've got a man in my office here who's pretty sure he recognises her as a girl who took a furnished flat in Kennington last August. Want to see him?"

"Do I not!" Moresby exclaimed. "Send him round here at once, will you? And I'd take it as a favour if you'd send one of your chaps with him, just to make sure he doesn't lose his way or get run over by a bus. I can't afford to lose him now."

"And we get first claim on the story?"

"As soon as I give the word. Certainly you do. But don't print anything till I've seen him and got in touch with you again."

"Right you are." There was the sound of muffled voices at the other end of the wire. "He says he'll be delighted to come round to you. I'll send one of my chaps along to introduce him."

Within twenty minutes the newcomer was seated in Moresby's room and being welcomed with all Moresby's most genial smiles.

"Very good of you to come forward, sir. Very good. Your duty, of course, but everyone doesn't do their duty always, as you know as well as I do. If they did, our work here would be a lot easier, I can tell you."

The newcomer, who had announced himself as Mr. Pringle, preened himself. He was a tubby little man with a red face and gold pince-nez, and his manner was as effusive as Moresby's own.

"Not at all, Chief Inspector. Not at all. Delighted to be of assistance, if I can be."

Moresby asked his questions.

It appeared that Mr. Pringle was a house-agent, carrying on business in Kennington. On the 23rd of July of last year, according to his books, a young woman had called at his office to ask if he had a furnished flat to let for a short period. He had, in a quiet street not far from the Oval; a top floor, with a bedroom, sitting-room, and kitchen-bathroom; rent, two-and-a-half guineas a week. The young woman said it would suit her very well and had taken it on the spot, for the month of August only. On the 1st of August she called at his office for the keys and had, presumably, taken possession.

"I see," said Moresby, rubbing his hands with pleasure. It had been on the 1st of August that Roland House broke up.

"Have you any idea what time she called for the keys on the 1st?"

"What time? Dear me, that's rather a poser. No, I'm afraid I can't. I'll ask my clerk if he can remember, when I get back, but—no, I couldn't say myself."

"Now, it was actually you who showed her over the flat, was it, sir? Not your clerk?"

"No, no. I showed her over myself. That is how I came to recognise her photograph."

Moresby produced a copy of the photograph in question. "Just take a look at this. It's clearer of course than the newspaper reproduction. Does that help you to recognise her any better, or not?"

Mr. Pringle studied the photograph. "Yes, this is her. Undoubtedly. Quite undoubtedly. I remember her quite well, because I thought at the time what a pleasant-looking, quiet girl she was, so different from the type one sees about everywhere nowadays. Dear me, yes, one hardly knows what our young women are coming to. Yes, a good likeness. Undoubtedly that is her. Undoubtedly."

"You'd swear to that, sir?"

"Without hesitation," said Mr. Pringle manfully.

"Did she give any references?"

"No; she said she would prefer to pay for the month in advance. She paid for the full four-and-a-half weeks."

"In cash, or by cheque?"

"In cash. We shouldn't have given a receipt the same day if it had been by cheque."

"And you, of course, imagined that she stayed there the whole month?"

"I imagined so, no doubt; though of course it was no business of mine whether she stayed or not, so long as she had paid the rent."

"It didn't make you at all suspicious when she never returned the keys at the end of the month?"

"But the keys were returned. I verified that before I left my office this morning. They were returned by post, on the 1st of September."

"Oh!" Once again Moresby was impressed by Mr.

Wargrave's attention to detail. "I suppose it's too much to ask if you kept, or even noticed the post-mark of the envelope?"

"Too much, Chief Inspector, yes, too much. Undoubtedly too much. I'm sorry."

"Well, sir, one could hardly have expected it. There was no letter of course with the keys?"

"I asked my clerk that very question. He said he thought there was a piece of paper with the words 'Keys of top floor, 40, Elfrida Road, returned herewith,' or something like that scribbled on it, but he couldn't say for certain. In any case the paper wasn't kept."

"No, of course not. But you never recognised the name, Mary Waterhouse, when you saw it in the papers?"

"Dear me, dear me," clucked Mr. Pringle, "I should have mentioned that. That was not the same name that she gave us, Chief Inspector. No, no. We have her down in our books as Miss Marjorie West. Quite different, you see."

"But the same initials," said Moresby with satisfaction. "That settles it: it's the same girl. Funny how they change their names but keep to the same initials. Suit-cases and hand-kerchiefs, I suppose. Let me see, now. Forty, Elfrida Road, Kennington. Is that right? And she had the top floor. Is there anyone else living in the house?"

"Oh, certainly. Both the first and the second floors are occupied, and the landlord and his wife live in the basement; that is, to the best of my recollection."

"Then I hope your recollection is correct, sir," said Moresby jovially, as he rose. "Well, I don't think there's anything more to ask you. I have your address if anything crops up. Good morning, sir, and I'm very much obliged to you for coming forward with this information."

Mr. Pringle was beamingly ejected.

Moresby sat down at his desk again and, with difficulty restraining the carol which was hovering on his lips, rang for Inspector Fox.

"The first bit of real information received we've had on the case yet," he glowed, when he had explained what had happened. "And a nice, soft job for you out of it. Take the girl's photo, and Wargrave's, go down to Kennington, and find out if any of the other people in the house recognise either of them. Then try the shops round, and all that. You know. And see if you can find out how long she was there, and the date she was seen last."

Fox nodded. "Yes, we might be able to establish the date of death on this. I'll see what I can do."

Left alone, Moresby began to write out an account of his interview with Pringle for the dossier, while it was fresh in his mind. It constituted, as he had said to Fox, the first really important information that had come to hand; and its consequences might be very large indeed.

He finished his report, sent it down to be typed, and leaned back in his chair.

It was almost impossible that Fox should have no luck this time. Moresby knew those tall houses converted into flats, where the landlord lives in the basement. There is very little that escapes the observation of those landlords and their wives. And when one of their floors is let to a single young woman, of attractive appearance, their vigilance is multiplied a hundred-fold. Jealous of their converted house's good name, zealous to smell out wrong where no wrong may be, these landlords are the self-elected vigilance committee of half middle-class London. No French concierge even can be fiercer in well-doing or more unwearied in nosiness.

Moresby pulled the telephone directory towards him, ruffled its pages, and found the number of Pringle, house-agent, Kennington. He asked for it.

Mr. Pringle, they told him with evident importance, was not yet back; he had gone out on urgent business, and...

"Yes, yes," said Moresby. "This is Chief Inspector Moresby speaking, from Scotland Yard. I've just seen Mr. Pringle. Is that his clerk?"

"Mr. Pringle's chief clerk is speaking," came the answer, in tones that spoke of a swelling bosom.

"Good. You know what Mr. Pringle has been seeing me about? Very well. I want to speak to the person who handed over the keys of 40, Elfrida Road to Miss Marjorie West on the 1st August last year."

"I did so myself, sir."

"You did, eh? Good. Can you remember her?"

"Very faintly. The photograph Mr. Pringle showed me in the *Daily Courier* certainly touched a chord in my memory, sir. Yes, I think I may say I have a distinct recollection of her now."

Moresby smiled as his imagination brought up the picture of the self-important little person at the other end of the line. "Good. By the way, what's your name, Mr...?"

"Worksop, sir. Alfred Worksop."

"Well, Mr. Worksop, I want you to throw your mind back and see if you can remember what time of day it was when Miss West called for the keys. Can you?"

In the pause that followed Mr. Worksop could almost be

heard hurling his mind back, to say nothing of the thud with which it landed.

"I may be wrong, sir, but I have a distinct impression that it was before lunch. Quite a distinct impression. But as to the exact time—no, I really can't tell you."

"Never mind. Before lunch is an important thing. What makes you think it was before lunch?"

"Well, sir, I seem to have an idea that I was about to offer to go round to Elfrida Road with Miss West—pardon! Miss Waterhouse, I should say—when something intervened to prevent me; and I fancy it may have been lunch."

"I see," said Moresby gravely. "It couldn't by any chance have been that she had a taxi outside, could it?"

"No, sir," said Mr. Worksop with decision. "The fact that she was in a taxi would not have prevented me from helping her to the best of my ability."

"But was there a taxi?"

"Now you mention it, Mr. Moresby, I believe there was. Yes, I'm sure there was. I remember her saying, could she have the keys at once as she had a taxi waiting."

"Ah! You didn't glance into the taxi, did you? I'm rather anxious to know whether there was anyone else inside it."

"There I cannot help you, sir. I almost certainly didn't glance inside the taxi. It would not have been a very polite action, would it?"

"Wouldn't it?" said Moresby vaguely. "Well, never mind; it's nearly as important for me to know that she had a taxi. Thank you, Mr. Worksop."

"At your service, sir," responded Mr. Worksop courteously, as he rang off.

Moresby pressed a button and sent a messenger to summon Sergeant Afford.

"Well, Afford," he grinned, "care to have another go at those Euston porters? Well, well, how that takes the mind back. 'Oh, those Euston porters: here they come, here they come, here they come!' When was the song? Nineteen-thirteen or thereabouts. Well, well."

Sergeant Afford eyed his chief in surprise. For Chief Inspector Moresby to carol during office hours betokened something portentous. "What news have you had, sir?"

"Wonderful detective, Afford, aren't you?" sneered Moresby. "Ought to be in a story-book, you ought. But I have had a bit of news for all that." He retailed his bit of news.

"So off you go back to Euston, my lad, and get hold of the regular taxi-men there, and see if you can find one who drove a young woman on the 1st of August last from Euston to Kennington—40, Elfrida Road, with a call at 207B, Kennington High Road on the way. Yes, I know we've tried to find the man before, but we hadn't got the Kennington end then; that may jog their memory. And if you can't find the man there, go the whole round as usual; and don't you show that ugly face of yours here again till you've found him."

Sergeant Afford returned the other's grin, and went off, uncomplaining.

As for Moresby, he went out to lunch.

It was at about half-past three that the last drop was added to Moresby's cup of joy for the day.

The telephone-bell on his desk rang, and Inspector Fox announced himself at the other end.

"Just ringing up before I tackle the shops, Chief. Thought you'd like to hear the good news."

"What good news? Get it out, man, and don't palaver so much."

A faint laugh came from the other end of the wire.

"The landlord recognises the girl all right. *And* the other one too."

"Wargrave?"

"Wargrave. He visited her there two or three times."

Moresby chuckled horribly. "We've got him now, my boy. We've got Mr. Smartie now."

CHAPTER XIV

By six o'clock that evening his two subordinates had reported fully to the chief inspector, in person. At last it seemed the luck had really turned. Sergeant Afford had found, without difficulty this time, the taxi-man who had driven Mary Waterhouse from Euston to Kennington, and that link was finally established. Like Mr. Pringle, the driver had been impressed by her personality, and remembered considering that Kennington was not nearly good enough for her. He remembered too the halt at the house-agent's, and altogether had proved a most satisfactory witness.

Inspector Fox had been no less fortunate. Apart from the great *coup* of the landlord's identification of Wargrave, he had established some useful facts elsewhere. Armed with Miss Waterhouse's photograph, he had tackled the neighbouring shops, with the result that no less than three persons, Mrs. Dairyman, Mr. Grocer, and Mrs. Baker, had definitely recognised her. (Two of these three, it may be noted, had already been almost certain of recognising the photograph in the newspapers, but had not "liked" to come forward. With such prejudices does unfortunate Scotland Yard have to strive.) Their tales were, substantially, the same. Miss Waterhouse had not opened an account; she had paid cash; she had come regularly, well, almost every day you might say, for about a week, and had then come no more. Mrs. Dairyman, Mr. Grocer, and Mrs. Baker had all wondered why.

"That fixes it," Moresby said with satisfaction. "We knew all right that the second week in August was the time, but this fixes it; and pretty near the beginning of the week too. But it doesn't *prove* it," he added, more ruefully. "Not that she was killed, I mean."

"No, it doesn't do that, Mr. Moresby," Inspector Fox agreed. "You can't say that just because she left off dealing with the local tradesmen, that means she was dead."

"And for that matter," added the chief inspector, "the proof that it was Mary Waterhouse's body at all isn't anything like as strong as I'd like. I can hear Wargrave's counsel pulling it to bits easily enough. We know it's all right; but will the jury?"

"Oh, come, Mr. Moresby. That's going back a lot."

"Well, that's how this case makes me feel. I suppose we are getting on, and I suppose we will hang Wargrave one day, and our luck does seem to have turned at last. But I wish," said Moresby brutally, "that he was under the ground and the whole thing finished." He frowned heavily. "Anyhow, it's up to Mr. Smartie now. We'll have him on the carpet to-morrow morning, and it won't be my fault if he slides off it this time."

The truth was that the chief inspector, though still elated by the progress that had been made, was no longer quite so carried away by it as he had been that morning. In the interview with Wargrave that was now inevitable he foresaw several nasty moments for that gentleman, but so long as he kept his head Moresby was very much afraid that the honours would still remain with him.

Wargrave did keep his head.

He made not the slightest objection to coming to Scotland Yard again. Greeting Moresby with a little nod and a completely expressionless face, he dropped into his chair, crossed his legs, folded his arms, and then lifted his eyebrows without having spoken a single word. Mr. Wargrave was quite evidently not going to give himself away by talking too much.

In the corner the constable sat with pencil openly poised.

Moresby began quietly. "Sorry to bother you again, Mr. Wargrave, but there are one or two points we still don't quite understand."

Wargrave grunted—as Moresby thought, derisively.

"That revolver, for instance. I understood you to tell me last time you were here that you didn't own a revolver?"

Wargrave said nothing.

"You were not speaking quite truthfully?"

Wargrave said nothing.

"Come, sir. I asked you if you were not speaking the truth when you told me you had no revolver?"

Wargrave spoke for the first time. "Am I under any necessity to answer you?"

"Necessity? Certainly not. But I suggest that it's very much to your interest to do so."

"How?"

"Because otherwise," said Moresby glibly, "we might form a misconception about you."

"You've done that already. However, I'll answer you. Yes, I lied when I told you I didn't possess a revolver."

"And why did you do that, Mr. Wargrave?" Moresby asked, in hurt tones.

"Precisely because of that misconception you've just mentioned," Wargrave replied curtly. "And that is also the reason why I hid it."

"And is it also the reason why you threatened Sergeant Johnson with it, sir?"

"Threatened Sergeant Johnson? What on earth are you talking about?"

"I understand that when the sergeant approached you in the field, you pointed your revolver at him—loaded in five chambers."

"Then you've another misconception to contend with," Wargrave sneered. "But I imagine that you can't really be so foolish as to understand anything of the sort. If your sergeant understood it, he's half-witted."

"You deny that you pointed the revolver at him?"

"The suggestion," said Wargrave, with a tight little smile, "is not merely untrue; it's silly."

"I see, sir. Thank you. Why did you hide the revolver?"

"I've just told you."

"Because you were afraid that we might have formed a misconception about you?"

"Precisely."

"I don't think I quite understand you, Mr. Wargrave. What misconception exactly did you think we had formed?"

"Come, Mr. Moresby," Wargrave mocked, in imitation of the chief inspector's own manner. "Don't be childish."

"Well, to be frank, then, you thought we suspected you of having a hand in Miss Waterhouse's death?"

"To be still franker," Wargrave said drily, "I knew you suspected me of having caused it."

"You're quite wrong, Mr. Wargrave. It's too early to suspect anyone yet."

"I'm glad to hear it."

Moresby began to scriggle on his blotting-paper. He was getting no further.

"I should like to know," he said slowly, "why you really hid that revolver, Mr. Wargrave?"

Wargrave shifted in his chair in an exasperated way. "How many more times am I to tell you?"

Moresby noted the sign of exasperation with satisfaction. He went on putting questions about the revolver: why Wargrave had denied the possession of it, why he had tried to hide it, what he had intended to do with it, why, why, why, putting the same query over and over again in only slightly different words. His plan was perfectly simple: to exasperate Wargrave to such a pitch that when he finally sprang the bombshell about Kennington the other would have so lost control of his nerves as to be startled into some vital denial. The tactics were perhaps not of the kind of which Superintendent Green would have approved, but Moresby was not bothered by that.

"Good God, man," Wargrave broke out at last, "how much more about this infernal revolver? I've told you and told you again. I refuse to answer another question about it."

Moresby judged that his time was ripe. "Very well, sir. If you refuse, you refuse. Then perhaps you'll tell me instead how many times you visited Miss Waterhouse at 40, Elfrida Road, Kennington, between the 1st of August last year and the 8th?"

No sooner had he spoken the words than he knew that he had lost the trick. Wargrave seemed to tighten suddenly all over. The look of irritation vanished from his face, to be replaced by its former expression of blankness. Moresby could not help admiring the man's self-control.

There was scarcely a pause before he answered, in flat tones: "I'm afraid I can't tell you exactly. Two or three times, I believe."

"You admit, then, that you did visit her there?"

"Of course."

"But I understood you to say last time you were here that you never saw Miss Waterhouse again after the end of last summer term?"

"You understood quite correctly. I did say so."

"You were not speaking the truth, then?"

"I was not."

"You were trying deliberately to mislead me?"

"I was."

"That was a very serious thing to attempt, Mr. Wargrave."

Wargrave said nothing.

"What was your reason?"

Wargrave gave his bleak little smile. "You know my reason well enough."

"I should prefer you to state it, if you care to do so; though I should warn you that—"

"Oh, I don't mind, if you want your man to take it down. My reason was that same misconception you spoke of just now."

"I see. You feared…?"

"Considering the ridiculous mistake you were so evidently making, I saw no reason why I should present you with any evidence which might seem superficially to support it," Wargrave almost dictated to the constable.

"You took this mistake of mine, as you call it, pretty seriously, then?"

"Well, it was what one might call rather a capital mistake, wasn't it?" Wargrave said grimly.

Moresby went on to the obvious question as to Wargrave's reasons for visiting Kennington, but it was a disappointed man who put them. His hope had been that Wargrave would have denied having visited Kennington at all. There would then have been identification parades, and all the usual ominous procedure; and things would have looked distinctly black for Wargrave. But Wargrave must have summed the situation up in one flash of thought, seen the danger, and avoided it. Moresby had the uneasy feeling that his mind was up against one more subtle, more intelligent, and more adamant.

Of course, Wargrave's explanation of his visits was both simple and, to anyone who might have believed in his innocence, convincing. He had paid his first visit to Mary Waterhouse for tea, by arrangement. She had told him about the flat she was taking, had said she would be lonely there, and had asked him to tea. At tea she had told him that one of the electrical standard lamps was defective. He had examined it, found that the socket was defective, and offered to get her a new one and fit it himself to save her the expense of an electrician. His second visit had been for this purpose. The third one had been no more than to return a book borrowed on the second occasion, a matter of a couple of minutes only.

And that was all? That was all.

"You seem to remember these trivial visits very accurately after so many months, Mr. Wargrave."

"A schoolmaster," returned Wargrave, "has to have an accurate memory for trivial details."

"Humph!" said Moresby, and did not conceal his scepticism. "What did you understand of Miss Waterhouse's plans for the future?"

"I gathered that she had taken the flat for the purpose of establishing a domicile in London, so that she and her *fiancé* could be married at the Kennington registry office without trouble as soon as he arrived in this country; which seemed to me a very reasonable thing to do."

"Her *fiancé* had not arrived then?"

"So she told me."

"It never struck you as odd that she should suddenly become engaged, in the middle of that term, to a man who was in Australia at the time and whom she couldn't have been seeing?"

"No. There is such a thing as a post."

"Nor that she should have acquired a ring, also from a man who could not have given it to her in person?"

"There's a parcel-post as well as a letter-post."

"The possibility never occurred to you then, Mr. Wargrave, that this *fiancé*, whose name even doesn't ever seem to have been mentioned, might not exist at all? That he might have been a pure invention of Miss Waterhouse's imagination?"

"I'm afraid it didn't. One doesn't usually ascribe one's friends' *fiancés* to their imaginations."

"To account for her condition?"

"I wasn't aware of her condition."

"In view of the evidence we have, which I mentioned to you the other day, it seems strange that you shouldn't have known of such an important matter?"

"I can't help that. Miss Waterhouse certainly did not pay me the compliment of confiding in me to that extent."

"I see. You had no suspicions at all, then, with regard to this *fiancé*?"

"None. Have you? I take it you can't find him, from the way you speak."

"We certainly haven't found him yet. Miss Waterhouse," said Moresby coolly, "had been blackmailing you?"

"What!" The start that Wargrave gave was genuine enough, but Moresby did not believe that it was a start of astonishment. He had dropped his question out of the blue with the purpose of watching Wargrave's reaction to it rather than of learning anything from his answer. For the first time during the interview the chief inspector was satisfied that he had taken the other off his guard. The start, he felt convinced, had been a guilty one, though the next moment the man had recovered himself as completely as ever. "I don't understand you," he said coldly.

"No? You knew of course that Miss Waterhouse was a bad character? That under various names she had served at least three terms of imprisonment before she went to Roland House?"

"I certainly knew nothing of the sort." Moresby, watching

closely, fancied he saw an expression of comprehension pass rapidly over Wargrave's face, as if this news explained certain matters which had before been obscure; and he fancied too that he knew what these matters were.

"It's a fact."

"Indeed?" said Wargrave, now with only polite interest. "How extraordinary."

"Very, to you, sir, no doubt. Now I have a note here that the last occasion on which you visited Miss Waterhouse at 40, Elfrida Road was on about August 6th or 7th. You can't make it more definite than that?"

"I'm afraid not."

"That was the last time you saw her?"

"Yes, and then only for a couple of minutes."

"You did not visit the flat again, without getting a reply?"

"No, I went home to Clitheroe within a day or two of those dates, and had no occasion to visit Miss Waterhouse again."

"That's a pity, Mr. Wargrave. If you had happened to visit her again, you see, especially by appointment, and got no reply, it would help us a lot towards establishing the date of death. Just think again, sir, if you please."

"I can't alter facts to help you, I'm afraid, Chief Inspector. I did not visit Miss Waterhouse again after I took her book back."

Moresby leaned across the table. "Then you met her by appointment elsewhere?"

"No."

"I see." Moresby stroked his chin for a moment, and then gave his interrogation another swift twist. "I believe, Mr. Wargrave," he said conversationally, "that you know all about building?"

"I'm not an architect, if that's what you mean."

"Perhaps I should have said bricklaying."

"I know how to lay bricks, certainly. As a matter of fact I've been teaching some of the boys at Roland House. But I wouldn't go so far as to say I knew all about it."

"But you can do a simple job of bricklaying as well as a professional bricklayer?"

"I should imagine so. It's very simple."

"Quite so. What proportions do you use, for the sand and cement?"

"That depends what work I'm doing. For ordinary walling, usually five to one; for pointing, one and one."

"And for laying a brick floor?"

"I can't tell you. I've never laid a brick floor."

"But if you were laying a brick floor?"

"If I were laying a brick floor on a proper concrete bed, I should probably use about four to one, but five to one would do just as well."

"And for a brick floor laid straight on earth, without any concrete bed?"

"I shouldn't do such a scamped job," replied Wargrave, with finality.

Moresby doubled on his tracks once more. "You say you bought an electrical fitting for one of Miss Waterhouse's lamps. Can you give me the name of the shop where you bought it?"

"No."

"You can't?"

"I'm afraid not."

"Ah!"

"But I can tell you where it was. It was an electrical and wireless shop in Grove Street, which is a turning off the Cromwell Road. I went there one afternoon at about half-past four, from the Science Museum, and then straight on to Kennington."

"I see." Moresby was a little taken aback. He had quite decided that the electrical fitting was a myth.

He tried one last throw.

"Will you tell me, Mr. Wargrave, for what purpose you accompanied Miss Waterhouse to Lewisham?" It was a question which as he very well knew, he ought not to have put, but he was getting desperate.

Wargrave smiled faintly. "I did not accompany Miss Waterhouse to Lewisham, Chief Inspector. So far as I know I have never been in Lewisham in my life. Quite certainly I have never been in Burnt Oak Road."

Moresby had no option but to let him go.

CHAPTER XV

Roger Sheringham had refused Moresby's suggestion that he should constitute himself a spy in the Roland House camp, but that did not mean that he was not interested in the case. On the contrary, his interest was acute. What helped to make it so was his conviction that Moresby was working on the wrong lines. Roger was sure that probe and ferret and delve as Moresby might, he would never unearth enough sheer evidence to justify the arrest of Wargrave. There were too, he felt, psychological possibilities about the case which Moresby had overlooked; and, as always, it was the psychological side which excited Roger much more than the purely evidential. He was as ready to work hard in the discovering of evidence of fact as any man from Scotland Yard, but almost always it was only to prove a psychological case. Roger felt very much inclined to tackle the problem of Mary Waterhouse's death on these lines.

Since their curtailed dinner at the Albany, Moresby had kept Roger informed of the progress that the case had made, and the latter learned of the abortive interview with Wargrave within a few hours of its occurrence.

"He was too much for me, Mr. Sheringham," Moresby admitted handsomely, "and that's a fact."

"You tackled him wrongly," Roger returned with severity.

"I did, did I? Well, what would you have done, sir?"

Roger thought hurriedly. What would he have done? Or what, at any rate, was good enough to say to Moresby that he would have done?

He laughed suddenly. "What should I have done?" he repeated into the telephone-mouthpiece. "I'll tell you, Moresby. I shouldn't have let him know that I was convinced of his guilt."

"But he's known that from the beginning."

"Then I should gently have fixed in his mind, without ever saying as much, that I had only been pretending to suspect him. In reality I suspected one of the others. Duff, we'll say."

"And what good would that have done?"

"This. You tried to frighten him, and failed. I should have tried to fill him with a great relief. Relief loosens the tongue far more than fear ever could. He might have become, for Wargrave, quite garrulous. At the least I should have expected him to let drop something of value to the investigation."

Moresby jeered. "It's my belief you don't know Mr. Smartie Wargrave as well as I do, Mr. Sheringham, for all your psychological fiddle-faddle."

"And it's my belief that I know him a good deal better," retorted Roger, hurt. "What's more, I've half a mind to prove it to you."

"All right, sir," Moresby said offensively. "You do so, and then perhaps I'll believe it too."

"Very well; I will," Roger threatened, and hung up the receiver.

At the other end of the line Moresby hung up his receiver too, with a broad smile. It was astonishing how easy it was to get what one wanted out of Mr. Sheringham by just a little diplomacy, and him supposed to be a clever man too. Of one thing Moresby was quite sure: he needed no psychological fiddle-faddle to know Mr. Roger Sheringham a good deal better than Mr. Sheringham did.

In his study Roger was frowning at the telephone, but his thoughts were no longer upon that innocent channel of a chief inspector's offensiveness. He was considering how to make good his threat.

The case against Wargrave, he knew, depended now on one link: evidence to connect him with 4, Burnt Oak Road. Without that he could never be arrested; with it, he was as good as hanged. Roger was quite certain that any such evidence would never be discovered.

What then?

One thing at any rate was quite sure: if the police could find no evidence to connect Wargrave with Burnt Oak Road, neither could he, and it would be a waste of time to try to do so. Roger felt relieved as he pointed this out to himself, for he certainly had no wish to attempt anything of the kind; his leanings lay elsewhere. It would be more amusing, for instance, to work on inductive lines and form a theory as to how Mary Waterhouse could possibly have been inveigled into that cellar, and then examine the possibilities of proving it.

Roger dropped into the chair by his desk, thrust his hands

deep into his pockets and his legs out straight, and gave himself up to a little solid concentration. How, if he himself had been in the murderer's shoes, would he have acted?

With a great many of Moresby's ideas Roger was in agreement. That Mary Waterhouse had been Wargrave's mistress, that she had made trouble over the coming child, that she had blackmailed him, were almost self-evident. That Wargrave's ambition all along had been to marry Amy Harrison and obtain the reversion of Roland House, he himself had seen. Undoubtedly Mary Waterhouse had seen it too, long before. Whether she had stipulated for marriage herself, or merely money and plenty of it too as soon as Wargrave got an interest in the school, was beside the point, though Roger was inclined to the latter supposition; what was certain was that her threat had been to tell Amy of her own relations with Wargrave. Amy would never stomach that. Wargrave would be finished there, his ambitions in that line knocked flat. What then should be Wargrave's retort to that? Murder?

"If I'd been Wargrave," thought Roger, "I should have held her off till I'd married Amy, and then simply told her to go to hell. After all, that's the obvious course."

He nodded to himself. That was the perfectly obvious course.

However, all this was beside the point. The question was: had Roger Sheringham, being a master at Roland House Preparatory School and undergoing blackmail at the hands of Miss Mary Waterhouse, determined to kill and murder the said Mary Waterhouse in a cellar in Burnt Oak Road, Lewisham, how the devil would he have got her there first?

But no. That was not the first question. It might be putting the cart before the horse to pose that question first. Primarily it should be asked: did the plan to murder Mary Waterhouse in the Lewisham cellar have its origin in the possibility of getting her there?

At once Roger saw that this was far more probable. The plan, in other words, had depended upon the cellar; not the cellar upon the plan. In that case, and assuming that this was so, the next question became: how did it come about that her murderer could lure Mary Waterhouse with such ease to a cellar in Lewisham?

Roger frowned. That seemed rather odd. One does not say to a young woman: "I know a good cellar. Let's go to it." Besides, according to Moresby's theory, which was really a very plausible one, the access to the cellar came from Mary Waterhouse herself, in the shape of Miss Staples's purloined key. In that case it should have been Miss Waterhouse who led the way to the cellar. What did that give? Why, a very interesting twist to the second question. In this light, and remembering always that there had been behind this murder an extremely clever brain, the second question then resolved itself into: how did it come about that Mary Waterhouse was induced to lead her murderer into that cellar? Or, to put it a little more concisely: what inducement had Mary Waterhouse to lead her murderer into that cellar?

Roger thrust his hands still deeper into his pockets, and gave a little wriggle of achievement. Put in that way, the question immediately suggested its own answer. To levy her blackmail!

That would indeed have been a master-stroke. The victim knows that the blackmailer has access to this cellar (how he knows it is beside the point for the moment; the knowledge must be assumed). By careful enquiry (again to be assumed for the present) he learns that the three houses of which this particular one is the centre will all be empty during the second week of August. He arranges matters so that an interview with the blackmailer is necessitated during that week. Then he drops hints, pretends to kick, speaks of other blackmailers who have been trapped by policemen concealed behind curtains, behind pillar-boxes, behind gorse-bushes, behind every conceivable object except the lumber in a total stranger's cellar, but never, never mentions the cellar in question. That is for her to think of, as her own discovery. And following the line of thought that he has mapped out for her, she does arrive duly at the cellar. The cellar; not the dining-room, or the drawing-room, or one of the bedrooms; but only where there is no possibility of raised voices being overheard by any chance prowler in the street outside—the cellar.

No, she would not arrive at the cellar so soon, of course. The empty house first. The cellar would be an improvement, once she was inside the house.

The more Roger thought of it the more convinced he became that this was what must have happened. Made nervous by her victim's references to curtains, pillar-boxes, gorse-bushes, and the traps of that kind, which can be set in a prearranged meeting-place, Mary Waterhouse becomes conscious of the plan which has been so deftly inserted in her mind. She arranges what shall look like a perfectly innocent meeting in some perfectly innocent place, and then leads her victim circuitously, and with proper precautions against being followed, to Burnt Oak Road. "Aha," she says, in effect, "now we've come to a place where I'm perfectly safe. We haven't been followed, and it's quite impossible that you could have anticipated my bringing you here. Now you can hand over that cash without the slightest danger to me of the action being overlooked by any spy of yours." And that is the end of Mary Waterhouse.

Very ingenious, thought Roger with admiration: and how else can it possibly have happened?

In fact there was only one difficulty in this reconstruction. How could the victim have known of the blackmailer's possession of the key?

Such knowledge almost inevitably implied knowledge too of the blackmailer's past. It was not enough that the past should have been deduced from the possession of the key. Even if Miss Waterhouse had let out the fact of her possessing it, she could have found a hundred innocent explanations to cover her slip. Never, surely, would she have deliberately divulged her own record. That meant that this knowledge on the part of the victim must have come from another source. Could it be that Mary Waterhouse herself had been undergoing blackmail? Roger knew that this very often happened in the case of a person with a prison record who is trying to go straight. If that were so, she must have failed to meet the demands of the blackmailer, who had handed on his information to the person whom he saw to be most intimately connected with the girl. Thus taxed, and with complete proofs in the hands of the man, she would probably have become brazen and not only admitted but boasted of her misdeeds; and so to the key. That all hung together. And this knowledge on the part of her own victim would not abate her demands upon him in the slightest degree; if anything it would increase them.

Yes, that, or something on similar lines, cleared up the only real difficulty that Roger could see in the theory. And the actual clearing-up offered a new source of possible profit to the enquiry: the circumstances surrounding the information laid against Mary Waterhouse. Certainly they must be examined, from every angle.

It was true that a minor difficulty still remained. The theory postulated enquiry on the part of Mary Waterhouse's murderer at Nos. 2, 4 and 6, Burnt Oak Road, regarding the summer holidays of the occupants; and Scotland Yard had been unable to trace any such enquiries as having been made.

Roger did not think that Moresby had worked here on quite the right lines. It was inconceivable that the murderer, who had shown himself so cunning in other ways, could have been so foolish as to have made these enquiries *in propria persona*. To take round a photograph of Wargrave and ask whether the inhabitants of Nos. 2 and 6 could recognise him, was useless. And the mention of any kind of disguise, such as horn spectacles, had apparently reduced Moresby to such hopelessness that he had done nothing more about it.

Putting himself again in the murderer's shoes, Roger felt that what he would have done would have been to impersonate some figure from whom an enquiry regarding the future would have been so inevitable as to remain unregistered on the memory. What sort of figure suggested itself? Well, something in the nature of a tradesman with goods to deliver ahead, or a jobbing workman who was full up this week, but could do a cheap job next week, such as a window-cleaner. Roger began to jot down a list of possibles, remembering as he did so that since the school had broken up on the 1st of August and the murder might have taken place on any day after the 7th, these enquiries must have been made during the first week of August, and almost certainly during the first half of it; moreover the probabilities were that they had been put not to the mistress of the house, but to its Mabel.

When he had written down all he could think of, he called Moresby on the telephone.

"I've got a little job for you, Moresby. Yes, in that affair you handed over to me. Send a man down to Lewisham with instructions to ask the maids at 2 and 6, Burnt Oak Road, whether they remember any of the following calling at the house during the first few days of last August and saying he could do a job cheap, or deliver some goods cheap, later in the month, and then never turning up again. Got that?" He read out his list.

"I see what you're getting at, Mr. Sheringham."

"I should hope so. You ought to have seen for yourself without my telling you. By the way, he was probably in disguise, don't forget. He may have been wearing a beard."

"Beards usually look false," Moresby said doubtfully.

"But not always. Ask Clarkson," said Roger, and rang off.

He leaned back in his chair again. It would be amusing, very amusing, if he really could beat Moresby for once at his own game again. He had not done so for a long time; not since that unpleasant affair connected with silk stockings. Moresby had been getting rather too much the expert lately. It was time to take him down a peg. And working as he was on the wrong lines in this case (for of that Roger was by now quite convinced), here was an excellent opportunity.

Very well, then; what was the next move?

He remembered his own words to Moresby as to how the interview with Wargrave should have been conducted: that it should have been conveyed to the latter that the suspicion against him was only pretended and that in reality it was directed against one of the other masters—Duff, for instance.

Was it too late to put that into practice on his own account? Well, there was no harm in trying. He would go down to Allingford and have an interview with Wargrave.

And there was no time like that same afternoon.

CHAPTER XVI

ROGER WAS PLEASED WITH HIS THEORY OF THE WAY IN which the murder had been brought about. The more he thought about it, and he thought about it all the way down to Allingford, the more sure he was that by sheer reason and elimination he had arrived at the truth. Unfortunately, however, it did not help him in the least towards the proving of his case. There was not a jot of solid evidence in the whole chain.

Nevertheless the work had not been wholly wasted, even in this respect. Passing again in review, very much more rapidly, the processions of thought which he had inaugurated that morning, he discovered one section of them to be blaring suddenly like a brass band. He had paid only scanty attention to it before. Now he realised that perhaps it might prove the wheeling-point of the whole case. It was with a mind still full of its possibilities that he walked slowly up the drive of Roland House, which he had not seen for nine months.

Out of courtesy he had to ask for Amy Harrison first, congratulate her on her engagement, and spend ten minutes talking inanities in the drawing-room. Roger noticed that during that time Amy did not once mention Mary Waterhouse, her murder, or a word about the flutter which the event must have caused in the household. An exceptional woman, thought Roger, not for the first time; and thanked heaven that it was not he who was booked to marry her.

Mr. Harrison, he was glad to hear, was engaged in his study. He excused himself, on the plea that Amy must be busy, and said he would stroll round to the masters' sitting-room and see if anyone were about. He was careful not to ask for Wargrave.

The masters' sitting-room was tenanted by Mr. Parker only, ensconced as usual behind *The Times*. He blew through his moustache a welcome, and plunged without hesitation into the topic of the moment.

During the next fifteen minutes Mr. Parker rendered himself liable for a singularly long term of imprisonment for criminal libel. His opinion about the case was distressingly clear, and he voiced it no less firmly. If it was to be taken as representing the opinion of Roland House *in toto*, the wonder was that Wargrave had the effrontery to stay on in the place. Mr. Parker said as much, with manly directness. He also added, with no less clarity, what he himself would have done had he sat in Mr. Harrison's chair. It was mainly connected with the toe of his boot and a certain portion of Mr. Wargrave's anatomy.

"And Rice?" said Roger, not without maliciousness. "He disagrees with you?"

Mr. Parker filtered the suggestion indignantly through his moustache. "Disagrees with me? Why the devil should he? Good fellow, Rice. Very sound fellow indeed. Young perhaps, but very sound. Great pity he's leaving us at the end of this term. Going to Cheltenham, you know; yes. Done the place a lot of good. 'Member those cricket teams of his, don't you? Excellent idea. Makes the boys keen. Yes, very sound fellow, Rice."

Roger marvelled gently.

Released from Mr. Parker's presence, he wandered out into the garden. The wall which had been in the making last summer term was completed. Roger looked at it thoughtfully.

Wargrave was not in the garden, and he was not on the playing-field, where Mr. Rice interrupted his refereeing of a game of rugger (hockey during the Easter term had been abandoned since Mr. Rice's arrival) to come to the touchline and offer Roger a hearty if muddy hand. He stayed for a few minutes, punctuating his repetition of Mr. Parker's words with bellowed objurgations of this player or that.

"You want to see Patterson, I expect?" he added. "Merriman, you ghastly idiot, why didn't you *pass*? Don't be so infernally selfish!—Well, it's not your lucky day. He's run up to town for the—Feet, stripes, use your *feet*!—What was I saying?—Here, forward, forward! Scrum down." His whistle blew vigorously.

Roger left him.

Wargrave was discovered at last, in the laboratory.

"Hullo," said Roger casually. "How are you, Wargrave? I've just run down to have a look round. I say, this is new, isn't it?"

Wargrave looked at him suspiciously from under his heavy brows. "Hullo, Sheringham," he answered, with neither hostility nor friendliness. "Yes, this is new."

"Very nice. Going in for science here seriously?"

"Harrison agrees with me that it will be just as well to offer a grounding in simple chemistry."

"That's something new for a prep. school."

"Yes."

The conversation looked like dying of inanition.

"By the way, congratulations on your engagement."

"Thanks."

Roger fiddled with a test-tube. "Doing anything important? Am I interrupting you?"

"Not in the least."

"I've just been down to the field. Rice seems to be going as strong as ever."

"Yes."

"I saw Parker in the masters' sitting-room. Haven't seen Duff yet."

"No?"

Damn the man, thought Roger; one might as well try to make pleasant conversation to a slop-pail.

He took the bull by the horns. "Well, and what do *you* think about Mary Waterhouse?"

"You've heard what Rice and Parker think?" Wargrave asked, quite without rancour.

"I have."

"Then you'd better not ask me. By the way, aren't you connected with the police or something?"

"Not connected with them, no. But I'm in touch with Scotland Yard, quite unofficially."

"Come down here to pump me?" Wargrave asked, with a dry smile.

"Yes," said Roger.

Wargrave's smile broadened a couple of millimetres. "Well, that's frank, at any rate."

"I believe in frankness. That's why I'm here this afternoon. Entirely on my own account, by the way, as an infernal busybody; nothing to do with Scotland Yard or anything like that."

"You find yourself interested?"

"Naturally; having known her—and you."

Wargrave raised his black eyebrows a fraction of an inch, but did not speak. He seemed to be waiting.

"Care to talk it over?" Roger asked, as casually as if the matter were what they should eat for dinner.

"I've nothing to say."

"On the contrary, you've got a great deal: if you like to say it."

"Are you asking me to incriminate myself?"

"No, exculpate."

"What exactly are you driving at, Sheringham?"

Roger thought rapidly for a moment. The great thing was to induce Wargrave to talk, no matter what line he took; whatever line he did take was bound to be interesting. By all spiritual laws he must be bursting to talk, however he might conceal it. Since the business began he could not have had any kind of a confidant. Even to Amy he could not have divulged the reason for the police and the general suspicions of him. And however self-contained and self-sufficient a man may be, in a time of great mental stress a confidant is the natural safety-valve. Surely Wargrave's mind must be nearing its explosion point.

The difficulty was to choose just the right lever with which to persuade it to open.

Roger made up his mind. "What am I driving at?" he said in his frankest tones. "I'll tell you, quite candidly. The police believe you shot Mary Waterhouse: I don't. I want to help you." It was a speech which even Moresby would have shrunk from uttering.

"Very kind of you," said Wargrave indifferently, leaning back against the benching. "But I really don't understand why you should wish to help me. Not that I need it, in any case."

"Well, put it that just for my own satisfaction I should like to show Scotland Yard that I'm right."

"To do that involves proving a case against somebody else. Is that what you mean?"

"Not necessarily," Roger said, making a note of the fact that Wargrave evidently had the decency not to wish this to be done, even to save himself. "You might have an alibi."

"Extending over several days? Well, I haven't. How could I have, if I was in London and at large?"

"Something of that nature, I mean, to show you couldn't have committed the crime."

"There's nothing to show that I didn't commit the crime," Wargrave replied drily. "On the other hand, there's nothing to show that I did. So why worry?"

"Damn it though, man," Roger exclaimed, irritated by this cold-blooded cynicism, "don't you even deny having committed it?"

"Of course I do. Do you expect me to admit it?"

"You seem to be tacitly almost admitting it."

"Then you misunderstand me," said Wargrave, with something approaching a yawn. "I admit nothing. I deny everything. Nothing will ever be proved, one way or the other.

The police know that as well as you and I do. I suppose they asked you to come down and see if you could soft-soap me. Well, you can't."

Roger fought down an impulse to break one of his own retorts over the man's head, and smiled. "I told you I'd come on my own account. I know it's difficult for you to believe, but it's true. What's more, I'm not going to lose my temper with you. If you don't want to talk to me about things, of course you won't. I don't want to force your confidences in any way."

"You won't do that, don't worry," Wargrave said grimly.

"On the other hand I'm quite prepared to give you mine. You didn't seem to believe me just now when I told you that I didn't think that you shot Mary Waterhouse, but that someone else did. I'll amplify that and tell you just what I do think. It's my belief," said Roger, with complete and shameless untruth, "that it was Duff who shot her."

If his object had been to startle Wargrave, it had certainly succeeded.

"Duff! Duff couldn't shoot a rabbit."

"Oh, couldn't he!" Roger retorted, with a knowing air.

"What do you mean? How can you possibly think it was Duff?"

"I'll tell you. This crime has struck me from the very beginning," Roger explained glibly and with what he hoped was sincerity, "as the crime of a weak man. There's evidence of that all through, apart from the fundamental fact of murder being a sign of weakness in itself—as I remember actually pointing out to the chief inspector of the C.I.D. in charge of the case. 'Moresby,' I said, 'murder is evidence of a weak character even when it's a case of blackmailer and victim,'" Roger quoted, with extreme inaccuracy; "'Wargrave is *not* a weak man; therefore he wouldn't have had recourse to murder.'"

"Oh! You said that, Sheringham, did you?" Wargrave had not the air of a man convinced.

"I did," Roger lied without a blush. "That's what I thought then, and that's what I still think."

"Good," said Wargrave. "I'm glad to hear it."

Roger looked at him hopefully, but even this striking tribute to his character did not seem to have moved him. A rock-like man, Wargrave.

He tried a fresh cast.

"That girl certainly took me in last summer. I thought butter wouldn't have melted in her mouth. The last person I should have suspected of being a professional crook. I wonder you had anything to do with her, Wargrave."

For the first time Wargrave showed some emotion. "Good heavens, you don't imagine I knew any more than you did, do you? Of course I didn't. I wouldn't have looked at her if I had."

"Not even when she began blackmailing you?"

Wargrave looked at him woodenly, but Roger made a gesture of impatience. "Oh, you needn't be afraid of admitting that. That's been perfectly obvious since the case began. Besides, anything you say to me here isn't evidence. There's no witness."

"Very well, then," said Wargrave, rather sulkily. "Not even when she began—blackmailing me. She did it very cleverly. Played the little innocent right up to the end.—Right up to the last time I saw her," he corrected himself hurriedly.

"When did you find out that she was a gaolbird, then?"

"Not till your friend the chief inspector told me in his office, yesterday morning."

"It was a shock to you?"

"Well, I was annoyed. With myself, in a way. I felt I'd allowed myself to be had." It was an interesting and, Roger felt, a typical reaction.

"She was a dangerous woman," he said slowly, "and no loss to the world, whoever—removed her."

"Duff, for instance," Wargrave sneered.

"Duff, for instance," Roger agreed gravely.

They looked at each other.

"Look here," said Wargrave, "sorry, but I've got some work to do."

Roger nodded. "All right. I want a word with Duff, in any case."

Wargrave looked at him again, hard. "Don't go and make a fool of yourself," he said harshly. "You know perfectly well it wasn't—Duff."

Roger did know perfectly well it wasn't Duff.

Even if he had wanted to talk to Duff, which he didn't, there was no opportunity at the moment. It was nearly half-past four, and Amy had reminded him that there would be tea at half-past four in the drawing-room. Not even Roger dared to be late for Amy's tea.

Phyllis Harrison was already in the drawing-room, and greeted him with her usual mischievous smile. Roger liked her, and the two were able to keep the conversation going naturally enough for the next half-hour in spite of the stilted amiabilities of Amy, the heavy silence of Wargrave, and the rather absent and mechanical courtesies of Mr. Harrison.

None of the other masters, nor Leila Jevons, was present; their teas were served separately.

Before he went Roger had a short talk with Mr. Harrison, in the latter's study. After all, he felt, when one wants information one may as well go to the fountain-head.

"A shocking business, this of Miss Waterhouse," he opened bluntly. The subject had been obviously taboo at tea.

"Yes, yes," mumbled Mr. Harrison, plainly a little taken aback. "Dreadful, dreadful."

"I've been in touch with Scotland Yard on the matter."

Mr. Harrison opened his watery blue eyes wide. "You, Sheringham? Ah, yes, of course; I remember. You occasionally do work for them, don't you? And is that why...?"

"Partly. But I'm not exactly working for them at present. In fact, I'm here quite on my own."

"Indeed? Yes. Tell me," said Mr. Harrison anxiously. "What do the police really think? Not, I hope, I sincerely hope, that...?"

"Well, I'm really not at liberty to say what they think."

"No, no. Of course not. I quite understand. But..."

"Yes."

"I mean, whatever the police may think, it is impossible not to realise what is thought here."

Roger was feeling his way over rather delicate ground. "Your daughter's engagement," he said carefully, "has not been broken off."

"No, no," Mr. Harrison agreed in relief at this tactful way of introducing the Wargrave *motif* without the Wargrave name. "No, she wouldn't hear of it. I felt it my duty... But no. She dismisses the rumours with contempt."

"And you?"

"So do I," averred Mr. Harrison stoutly. "So do I. Certainly. It's unthinkable."

"Murder always is unthinkable."

Mr. Harrison winced slightly. "I suppose," he said feebly, "it could not possibly have been suicide? I—I know very little about the details."

"Quite impossible."

"No," said Mr. Harrison. "No."

"Why did you think it might be? I mean, why do you think she might have killed herself?"

"Her condition…"

"Girls don't kill themselves for that nowadays."

"No," Mr. Harrison agreed at once. "No."

"You had no other reason for thinking she might have committed suicide?"

"I?" said Mr. Harrison, not without signs of confusion. "Indeed no. How should I?"

"Why not be frank with me, Mr. Harrison? It can certainly do Wargrave no harm; it may do him quite a lot of good."

"I—I don't understand what you mean, at all."

"I think you do," Roger pressed him gently. "Shall I hazard a guess? Information reached you somehow or other, during that summer term, that Mary Waterhouse was a bad lot, an ex-gaolbird and all the rest of it. You privately gave her notice, but allowed it to be understood that she had resigned and let her put about the myth of the Australian *fiancé*. That is what is in your mind, isn't it?"

Mr. Harrison was staring at him with open mouth. "She *did* tell him then?" he managed to ejaculate.

"I was right?" Roger crowed. It had been a sheer inspiration of the moment. "Information to that effect did reach you?"

"I—I had an anonymous letter," faltered Mr. Harrison, almost as if detected in some crime himself. "I taxed her with the contents. At first she denied it. Then she—she broke down and admitted that it was true. I—I told her that she would have to leave. You don't think, Sheringham, that...?"

"No, no," Roger soothed. "That had no bearing on her death. It most certainly wasn't suicide."

"Ah!"

"And you told Wargrave about the contents of the letter?"

"Certainly not," Mr. Harrison repudiated with energy. "No, certainly I didn't."

"Whom did you tell?"

"No one. No one at all."

"Humph!" Roger stroked his chin. "An anonymous letter. Did you destroy it?"

"Not immediately. I thought..."

"Where did you keep it?"

"In my desk here."

"Locked up?"

"I—I don't think so. I don't really remember. Sheringham, I don't understand what you..."

"Never mind," Roger soothed him again. "I was only wondering who had access to your desk."

"If you mean that anyone would have come prying among my private papers, I must say at once that such a thing would be quite out of the question here. Quite."

"Yes, yes. Well, never mind. It's interesting, that's all. You're sure you haven't got the letter still?"

"No, no. I threw it away after Miss Waterhouse had left."

"I see. That's a pity. But you couldn't know, of course, could you? Still, I wish you could remember whether you had it locked up or not." Roger looked at the desk. "You do keep some of those drawers locked, I take it?"

"I keep one locked." Mr. Harrison hesitated. "I may have slipped the letter into it. I really can't say. Is it so important?"

"No, no; it doesn't matter. Well, I must be getting along. It's been good of you to let me have this talk with you, Mr. Harrison, but I mustn't take up any more of your time. I know how busy you are at the end of term. Oh, there is just one thing. You remember the school group that was taken while I was here last year? Somehow I never got a copy. I suppose you haven't got a spare one you could let me buy, have you?"

"I have a spare one, but I won't let you buy it," said Mr. Harrison, in obvious relief at the termination of the interview. "I shall be delighted to make you a present of it. Let me see now: I fancy it's upstairs. If you'll wait a minute I'll get it."

"That's very good of you indeed," Roger returned politely.

Mr. Harrison bustled out of the room.

Roger wondered how he could make use of his opportunity. Mr. Harrison had seemed very vague altogether about that anonymous letter. Was it possible that he had not thrown it away after all? If he had not, Roger would have very much liked to get hold of it; but of course it would be useless to ask for it outright.

By the direction of Mr. Harrison's glance it had been plain which was the locked drawer. Roger bent and glanced at the lock. Then he drew a small bunch of innocent-looking keys from his pocket, chose one, and inserted it. The lock was a simple one and turned at once. Roger opened the drawer. There confronted him inside not an anonymous letter but a very French photograph.

"Why," Roger asked himself, as he hastily shut and relocked the drawer, "do so many elderly men possess such nasty minds?"

CHAPTER XVII

ROGER WAS VERY MUCH PLEASED WITH HIMSELF. HIS visit to Roland House had achieved even more than he had hoped. Apart from anything else Wargrave, for instance, had admitted his intrigue with Mary Waterhouse and the fact that she had blackmailed him. Wargrave had known of course that anything he said to Roger in such circumstances could not be used as evidence, and that was why he had said it. Roger was really not surprised. He had guessed that Wargrave might let out something of that nature.

There were other things too. The anonymous letter was the most important of course. That was a striking confirmation of Roger's reasoning that same morning. Information had been laid against Mary Waterhouse, just as he had seen that it must have been laid. Roger was not at all sure that the anonymous letter was not going to clinch his case.

He got back to the Albany to learn from his man that Chief Inspector Moresby had been on the telephone half an hour ago, and had left word for Mr. Sheringham to ring him up the next morning.

Mr. Sheringham rang him up the next morning.

"Well, we've got something from that enquiry you put through yesterday, Mr. Sheringham," said Moresby. "I had it made on rather broader lines than you suggested, because I thought you might have overlooked one or two possibilities."

"Yes?" said Roger, a little coldly.

"Well, it wasn't him at all. It was the girl."

"The girl!" Roger repeated, surprised.

"You didn't expect that, Mr. Sheringham?"

"I didn't," said Roger, thinking ruefully of his beautiful theory.

"Well, I think we can bank on it. The maid remembers at No. 2 a young woman coming round just before the house was shut up last summer with an offer to make loose covers for armchairs. She had some patterns with her too. The maid remembers it, because the girl quoted prices that seemed even cheaper than the cost of the materials."

"They will overdo it," Roger murmured.

"Yes. Mrs. Cottington was out, and the girl—"

"Probably watched her go out."

"Yes. Anyhow, she said she'd come back that afternoon, but she never did."

"Ah!"

"Yes, you got that bit all right, Mr. Sheringham."

"She questioned the maid, I suppose?"

"Yes. They talked a bit about when the work could be done, and the maid remembers saying that it wouldn't be any good trying to fit them during the next couple of weeks because there wouldn't be anyone there."

"What about No. 6?"

"They don't remember anything about her there; but I don't think she ever called there. The maid says she asked whether it would be any good calling, and though she doesn't remember anything being said about it I expect the Waterhouse girl got it out of her when they'd be away too."

"The maid identifies her?"

"Half and half. She was wearing spectacles, and the maid *thinks* it might have been the girl in the photograph now. Before she swore she didn't recognise it at all. This bit about the loose covers has jogged her memory."

"Good," said Roger. "You could do with a few more jogs like that in this case, Moresby. Try and think some up for yourself next time."

Before he had hung up the receiver he had realised the mistake he had made in his reasoning before. It was a bad mistake. The reconstruction he had formed had really assumed knowledge on the part of both the man and the girl that Miss Staples's house and its neighbours were empty. He had not realised this, considering it enough that only the man need know. But how could the Waterhouse girl have taken him there at all unless she knew too?

Did that mean that the whole theory must be abandoned? Certainly it had been rather over-subtle. The truth probably lay somewhere near it. In any case it was obvious now that the girl had told him of the situation regarding the three houses. She would be hardly likely to do this if she wanted to keep the end of their journey a secret from him; which meant that she could not have taken him there for the purpose of levying her blackmail. Well, that hardly mattered. There were plenty of other reasons why they might have gone. It was, after all, a detail that did not matter in the least. The point was that they must both have known that the houses would be empty, and both have had their reasons for wanting to make use of that belonging to Miss Staples. His reason was murder; hers was now irrelevant.

Roger realised, although Moresby had not mentioned it, that this new piece of information would be a disappointment to the chief inspector. It meant the destruction of his last hope of connecting Wargrave with Burnt Oak Road. Except for the possibility of fresh evidence cropping up from some new source, a contingency most unlikely after all this time, Moresby must now have abandoned all expectation of bringing Wargrave to justice.

In that case, he thought, it did not really matter much what he himself did.

So he rang up Wargrave, and asked him to dinner.

"Dinner?" Wargrave said, in obvious surprise. "Sorry, impossible. I'm on duty here."

"Your prep.?"

"Yes. In any case—"

"In any case," said Roger firmly, "you'll come to dinner with me here this evening. You can go back by the 11.40. Don't tell me you can't get leave off for an evening when you want it, now." He slightly emphasised the last word.

"When I want it, perhaps," Wargrave said drily. "But as it happens—"

"Look here," Roger interrupted, "I'll say just this to you now. A certain chief inspector whom we both know has almost certainly given up all hope of laying by the heels a certain party. I haven't. In fact I've got quite a lot of new evidence which will come as a nasty surprise to someone. But before I hand it over to our friend, I want a talk with *you*. Now will you come to dinner?"

There was a long pause at the other end.

"Yes," said Wargrave.

"I thought you would," Roger said, with the greatest cheerfulness. "Get here about half-past seven. That will give us time for a glass of sherry. Don't bother to dress."

He rang off and went out to the kitchen of his flat.

"Meadows, I've just asked a friend to dinner to-night. I want you to give us a rather *macabre* little meal."

"I beg your pardon, sir? A what little meal?"

"*Macabre*. Gruesome. Horrible. Shivery."

"I don't think I quite understand, sir."

"Never mind, then," said Roger. "But it's a pity. I do think something *macabre* is rather called for."

If Meadows was unable to rise to any *macabre* heights concerning the food that evening, there was a distinctly *macabre* feeling in the air. Wargrave contributed to it. Really, thought Roger, the man did look like a murderer, with that sullen face and those black eyebrows and the hair that grew so low on his forehead, which always produces a sinister effect. Roger regarded his guest with pride. It was the first time he had entertained an almost self-confessed murderer to dinner—though he could not help wondering how many times he might have entertained a murderer unawares. It was a theory of Roger's that out of every score of people one knows, one at least is an undetected murderer. It was an hypothesis for which there was no evidence whatever, but it gave Roger a good deal of foolish pleasure in trying to pick out the twentieth ones in question.

Wargrave spoke little, answering his host's chatter about books, plays, and the like in little more than monosyllables. If he was apprehensive, he did not show it. As Moresby had already had occasion to observe, the man's self-control was abnormal. Roger hugged himself as he watched him. Wargrave was a new type to him. He was being cruel to the fellow, he knew; but why not? A little cruelty would do Wargrave no harm.

It was not until dinner was over, and the port on the table, that Roger introduced the subject of the meeting. All through dinner he had been waiting to see if Wargrave would introduce it himself, but not a word had he said that even hinted at such a thing. And yet he must have been waiting on tenterhooks for the other's explanation of his open threat over the telephone in the morning.

"Well, Wargrave," Roger said suddenly, breaking off a conversation concerning the shortcomings of English preparatory schools in the matter of the teaching of science. "Well, Wargrave, what does it feel like to have committed a successful murder?"

Wargrave looked at him unmoved. "I haven't committed a successful murder."

"Don't be modest. I should call it a very successful one. But for a piece of shocking bad luck it would never have been found out at all. But you didn't leave it at that. You took care that even if the impossible did happen and the body was found, there would be no evidence to prove a case against you. I do congratulate you, really."

"I haven't committed murder at all."

"Well, execution, then; or whatever you choose to call it. You needn't be suspicious, by the way. There's no one from Scotland Yard concealed behind the window-curtains, and there's certainly no dictaphone hidden under the table. Search the room, if you like."

"This is extremely good port, Sheringham."

"I'm glad you like it. But I wish you'd talk to me about things. You know murder's my hobby. I don't get a chance of hearing a real murderer discuss his crime every day, you know. In fact, you're the first one I've ever met in person. Why be so selfish?"

"I thought it was you who wanted to say things to me."

"Well, I have one or two points to put before you, it's true. But will you answer me a few questions first?"

"Depends what they are," Wargrave said nonchalantly, sipping his port.

Roger leaned back in his chair. "Well, the first one is this: how long are you going to keep this up?"

For the first time Wargrave shot a suspicious look at his host.

"Keep what up?" he asked.

"That you killed Mary Waterhouse."

"I didn't kill her."

"I know you didn't. So do you. So does one other person. But we three are the only people who do know it. And what I want to ask you seriously is: is it worth it?"

"Is what worth what?" Wargrave's tone was definitely uneasy at last.

"Is it worth pretending you did, in order to shield this other person? There've been no consequences yet, to speak of. But they're bound to come. At present it's only rumours, and the cold shoulders of your colleagues. But do you think it's going to stop at that? You're bound to be ruined, man. It's almost an open secret already. You'll have to leave Roland House; you'll never get another job; and—you'll have to break off your engagement, if you're to be logical. I mean," said Roger, picking his words more carefully, "if you're to carry the thing through logically."

"Look here, Sheringham, I simply don't know what you're talking about."

"Oh, yes, you do."

"I've told you I didn't kill the girl. You seem to think I know who did."

"I know you know who did."

"If it's this ridiculous idea of yours about Duff…"

"I'm not thinking about Duff at all. I never did think about Duff. That was a piece of bluff, to see how you'd react. I'm thinking about the person who really shot Mary Waterhouse. You know who that is, as well as I do—and better."

Wargrave was fiddling with the stem of his wine-glass. His face had gone perceptibly whiter.

"Look here, Sheringham, I don't know what extraordinary idea you've got in your mind," he said, his voice not quite steady, "but if you really are suspecting some quite innocent person… I have your word that we're not overheard here?"

"Absolutely."

"All right, then; it doesn't matter what I say. I *did* shoot her."

"Ah!" Roger breathed.

"You've been damned clever to get it out of me, because

I still don't know whether you're bluffing or not," Wargrave said, in tones of resentment. "But you can't do anything even now. It isn't evidence. You can tell the police what you like. I shall simply deny it."

"Of course," Roger approved. "Naturally."

Wargrave glowered at him in silence.

"Have some more port," said Roger, and passed the decanter.

"So what's this new evidence of yours?" Wargrave asked at last, as he refilled his glass.

"It alarms you that I've got some new evidence?" Roger asked, with interest.

"Not in the least. It can't be anything definite, or the police would have found it themselves. You needn't think you frightened me this morning. I know perfectly well I'm safe. I shall never be arrested."

"No?"

"Never," Wargrave said firmly. "They couldn't possibly get a conviction. We all know that." He smiled his tight little humourless smile.

"Well, I must say you're a cool devil," Roger admired.

"I haven't lost my head, if that's what you mean."

"Except over the revolver, perhaps."

Wargrave frowned. "Yes, that was a silly move. I had the wind up that day. However, it really didn't matter."

"As you took care to remove the bullet. If you hadn't done that…"

"But I did, you see. So far as I knew," said Wargrave frankly, "I made none of the usual foolish mistakes. You were quite right in what you told us that evening, Sheringham. Murder really is a very simple matter, to anyone of ordinary intelligence." He leaned back in his chair and smiled again, this time with something approaching triumph.

Roger watched him, fascinated. "Ah, you remember that?"

"Certainly I do. It made a very deep impression on me at the time."

"You find it a relief to talk openly, at last?"

Wargrave considered. "Yes, I think I do. I—well, I've had some bad moments, as you can imagine."

"Yes. And talking of imagination, you've got a lot more of it than I should ever have given you credit for, Wargrave."

"Oh? How do you make that out?"

"I think it must take a great deal of imagination to carry through a successful murder. That point didn't occur to me when I was saying how simple it was. It isn't really, at all. The number of things you must have had to foresee and guard against is tremendous."

"Oh, well..." said Wargrave, modestly.

"You don't mind answering a few questions?"

"I don't think so. Ask them, anyhow."

"Well, it's a psychological point really that's been puzzling me most. How on earth did you induce Miss Waterhouse to go to that house with you? I assume, by the way, that the choice of the house resulted from her possession of the key, and that she'd told you of her enquiries down there, from which she'd learnt that those three houses would all be empty during the second week in August?"

Wargrave nodded. "Yes, that's quite right."

"Well, how did you persuade her to take you there?"

"I'm not sure," Wargrave said slowly, "that I'd better tell you that."

"Why not? I give you my word not to pass it on. I'm only asking for personal curiosity. Besides, it can't do you harm in any case."

Wargrave seemed to be debating this. "Well, it was her idea."

"That both of you should go there?"

"Yes."

"You knew she'd been a crook?"

"No, I didn't know that."

"Then how did she explain her possession of the key?"

"Oh! Well, she said it was her aunt's house."

"What reason did she give for taking you there?"

"Oh, I don't know. Nice empty house, you know. Convenient, and all that."

"But why need a nice empty house when she'd got a flat where you could go to her?"

Wargrave hesitated. "There were reasons."

"You mean, she suggested on the spur of the moment that there was a nice empty house to which she had access: why not go?"

"Well, yes; that's pretty well what did happen."

"You hadn't intended to kill her, then? It was quite unpremeditated, when you found what a magnificent opportunity had been presented to you?" Roger asked excitedly.

Wargrave nodded. "You've about hit it, Sheringham."

Roger thumped the table. "You conveniently having a revolver in one hand, and a suit-case of mixed sand and cement in the other, I suppose? Wargrave, I was perfectly right. You haven't got so much imagination after all."

"What do you mean?" Wargrave asked, looking alarmed.

"Why, that we've had about enough of this farce. I've given you every chance to prove that you shot Mary Waterhouse, and you can't do it. Of course you can't. And why? Because, as both of us know perfectly well, it wasn't you who shot her at all."

"Then who was it?" Wargrave asked defiantly.

"Harrison," said Roger.

CHAPTER XVIII

WARGRAVE SEEMED AT LAST TO HAVE ACCEPTED DEFEAT.

"Well," he said slowly, "what are you going to do about it?"

"That depends rather on you. If you want to go about telling the world that you're a murderer in order to shield that old reprobate, I suppose I can't stop you. But at any rate I'm going to reason with you."

"What made you fix on Harrison?"

Roger crossed his knees and pushed his chair a little farther away from the table. "Psychologically," he began, in somewhat didactic tones, "there were only two men at Roland House who could have committed that murder. Subconsciously I realised that from the first, but I was carried away by the weight of the apparent evidence against you. It was a particularly cowardly crime, and it was carried out by a particularly cunning man. You might have fitted the second bill; but you didn't fit the first. It's perfectly true, as I said to you yesterday afternoon, that I told Moresby that murder is an act of weakness and it puzzled me that you should have descended to it. Finally I decided that you didn't."

"In spite of the evidence?"

"In spite of the evidence, which after all was mainly evidence of opportunity and motive only. I also decided that out of the Roland House staff Parker hasn't got the nerve, Rice hasn't got the originality, and Patterson just simply was out of the question. Only Duff or Harrison were weak enough men to shoot an unsuspecting girl from behind; and somehow I couldn't believe it of Duff. On the probabilities of character, Harrison was the most likely suspect for such a pusillanimous, feeble-minded, rat-in-a-trap murder as this. Do you agree with me so far?"

"It seems to me a long way from saying that a man had the sort of mentality which would lead him to commit a particular kind of murder, to saying that he actually did it. That kind of argument wouldn't appeal much to the police."

"The police!" echoed Roger with scorn. "The police are only interested in the kind of argument that will lead to a conviction. I don't care a bit about convictions. All that interests me is to get to the bottom of a problem and prove it to my own satisfaction. What happens to the murderer later isn't my affair, or my concern."

"I see," said Wargrave. "Well?"

"About Harrison, yes. Now I'm not a complete fool at summing a man up, Wargrave. After all it's a large part of my real job. And I was rather impressed with the fact that in a novel I began about you people at Roland House I made the character who was founded on Harrison take advantage of a situation in which a girl could hardly refuse him, to kiss her. I don't suppose for a moment that it ever actually happened. The point is that I saw Harrison even then as that kind of man."

"Yes?" said Wargrave, looking a little puzzled.

"Oh, it's an important point. It fits in this way. Thinking the case out, I arrived at the conclusion that the murderer *must* have known of Mary Waterhouse's past. You said you didn't, and I believed you didn't; and that confirmed my idea of your innocence. Harrison let out to me the fact that he did; and that confirmed my suspicion of his guilt."

"Harrison knew about her?"

"Yes. He had an anonymous letter, giving her record. Quite a common thing, I believe, in the case of one who has a record of that kind. Well, apart from this letter corroborating my notion that someone at Roland House must have known of Mary Waterhouse's past, it had another importance. It almost tells us in plain speech how the intrigue between Harrison and Miss Waterhouse began, doesn't it?"

Wargrave shook his head. "I don't see that."

"I was right about your lack of imagination," Roger said with interest. "You could never have put that crime through, Wargrave; and no one but the police could think you did. But about Harrison, does it help you if I tell you that on prying into a private drawer in his desk yesterday, I saw a really unpleasant photograph, lying on top of a pile of obviously similar ones?"

"You may be right that I have no imagination, or you may not," Wargrave said slowly, "but no, that doesn't help me at all."

"Then I'll explain. Harrison is quite obviously suffering from repression. I don't think that's difficult to understand. His wife certainly doesn't care for him; more, I should say she actively dislikes his attentions. I think it's very probable that Harrison knows about the affair between her and Rice, though it's equally probable that he's shutting his eyes to how far it may have gone. A *mari* semi-*complaisant*, through fear."

"Fear?"

"Yes, he knows that both Rice and his wife are stronger characters than himself, and he's afraid of both of them, just as he's afraid of his own daughter. And being a weak man, he is no doubt obsessed with the idea of 'getting his own back.' And I'll say at once that nine-tenths of that is Mrs. Harrison's fault.

"Well, understand the situation. There's Harrison, all agog; and there's this anonymous letter, which puts the girl apparently right into his power. What does he do? He has her in, taxes her with it, and gives her notice. She weeps, says she has been genuinely trying to turn over a new leaf (as I believe she genuinely had), and begs for another chance. All right, says Harrison, you shall have your chance, and stay on here, *if*... And she, having not much option, gives in.

"Now that's a very bad thing for both of them. The girl sees that it doesn't pay to try to go straight, and she gets more and more embittered. Quite naturally she relapses into her old frame of mind, the old frame of mind of the professional criminal, of being at war with society. And the first person she makes war on is Harrison himself.

"Harrison, in other words, finds he's caught a Tartar. Or rather, that the Tartar has caught him. She begins to blackmail him—and he has to pay up. It's about the only case I've met of the victim thoroughly deserving his blackmail. Then the child comes along, and there she is with both Harrison and you on separate strings, stinging both of you to her heart's content, and making each of you believe that you're the father of it."

Wargrave took a sip of port. "You're a bit wrong there," he said, without emotion.

"Eh?"

"There was never anything of that kind between Miss Waterhouse and me."

"What? But she was seen going into your room. That's what clinched the police suspicions against you."

"I know. That was rather funny," Wargrave said, without amusement. "She tried, but I wasn't having any. I shooed her out again in double-quick time, I can tell you."

"Oh! But the place was full of rumours about the two of you."

"Oh, yes. I liked the girl. I must admit I hadn't the least idea she was that sort. I did go up to London with her once or twice, but there was nothing in it; not even a flirtation. I'm afraid you've been misled by the natural feminine tendency to exaggerate these things."

Roger looked at him shrewdly. Naturally, Wargrave would not say that he had paid these small attentions to Miss Waterhouse for the express purpose of bringing Amy Harrison up to scratch. Roger was quite sure that such was the truth; but in any case that had nothing to do with the present subject.

"Well, I'm glad to hear it," he said. He accepted without hesitation Wargrave's word. "I certainly did think it was a little low to have been playing about with that girl, when your serious intentions lay in quite another quarter." Wargrave looked up sharply, but Roger went on without hesitation. "I should have known you better. But there again, why do you let people think it? You admitted to me yesterday straight out that she'd been blackmailing you."

"Thought I'd better," Wargrave growled. "You were getting a bit too near the truth for my liking."

"Well, we'll talk about that later. What we've got, then, is Mary Waterhouse blackmailing Harrison for all she's worth. Seeing the type of man she had to deal with, she probably made her demands not merely greedy but unreasonable. I can see her having no mercy on him. She knew she had him in a cleft stick. I don't know what she threatened, but it must have been complete exposure; and I shouldn't be at all surprised if her demands didn't include divorce of Mrs. Harrison on account of Rice, and marriage for herself. She knew, you see, that a schoolmaster simply can't afford scandal.

"But like most women, she overdid things. She was confident, and it never occurred to her that Harrison could turn on her to the point of murder. And yet to Harrison, distracted as he was, murder must have seemed the only way out; and if you brood long enough on a thing it becomes possible of achievement, even murder. Harrison, then, we may say, decided on Mary Waterhouse's murder, and only waited for a plan and an opportunity. And with both, as I see it, she must have presented him herself.

"How the subject of her key to 4, Burnt Oak Road, came up, of course it's impossible to say; but that doesn't really matter, because come up it obviously did. Harrison sees his chance. By careful preparation he plants in the girl's head the idea of using it as a meeting-place, and she goes off (probably thinking the plan is her own) to find out when it will be empty, as it is almost sure to be during the month of August. I can make a guess at Harrison's line. He has installed her in this furnished flat in Kennington, from which she can disappear later without comment, but he won't visit her there; he has no intention of being recognised later, as you were, if the unexpected happens and she is traced. Therefore they must have some other meeting-place. He vetoes all her suggestions about hotels and so on, until she hits on the bright idea, as he meant her to do all along, of 4, Burnt Oak Road. This is all theory, of course, but something like that must have happened.

"So they arrange to go there on a certain evening, after dusk. Probably they are to meet there, and Harrison takes with him a suit-case or some similar receptacle filled with his sand and cement, which he hides in the front garden; or of course he may have parked it there earlier. Naturally he doesn't go by taxi, which is traceable. There's a bus route just round the corner, you know. He'd only have to carry the heavy case a matter of fifty or sixty yards. And he takes with him your revolver, of the existence of which he is aware."

Wargrave nodded. "I used to keep it there. I never made any secret of it. It was always there in the holidays. But I didn't keep it loaded."

"No. But you had ammunition for it?"

"Yes."

"Exactly. Well, then he shot her," said Roger baldly. "Removed her clothes, leaving her gloves for the super-subtle idea of misleading the police about her rings, buried her, and bricked her neatly up. He'd learnt enough bricklaying for that job from watching you, of course."

"He took a hand in it once or twice," Wargrave amplified. "To encourage the boys, he said."

"Better still. Then he puts her clothes into the cement suit-case, and goes off, not knowing he's made the terrible mistake of not stamping down the earth tightly enough round the body. That," said Roger judicially, "was the only flaw in an otherwise perfect murder. Without that, the thing would never, never have been discovered.

"By the way, all this must have taken a considerable time. I think, if one were to make enquiries, that it might be possible to discover that Harrison had a night during the second week in August for which he couldn't account."

Wargrave shook his head. "No. You're wrong. He's got his alibi. What he must have done is to have left the girl there, gone back to his club where he was staying for part of that week, and slipped out again unseen to finish the job. He'd have a key, you see, and there would be no night-porter."

Roger looked at him. "Hullo, you've been doing a little investigating on your own account, have you?"

"Just that. And a very little at the house. I found the suit-case. You were quite right about that. It had distinct traces of cement in it still. I burnt it, in the school furnace."

"The devil you did! When did you know that it was Harrison, then?"

"The very moment I heard that the dead girl was Mary Waterhouse," Wargrave said calmly. "I'd got an idea of things before she left last summer term, you see. Nothing definite, but I heard her in the study on the last day of term speaking to him in a tone which made me jump. Of course, I didn't know he'd murdered her; I thought he must have bought her off.

Then when I realised what must have happened I went and saw him, while your chief inspector was interviewing Parker, and told him that I didn't know anything, or want to know anything, but all he'd got to do was to keep his mouth shut. I knew as early as that, from the chief inspector's manner, that I was under suspicion; and I knew they could never prove a case against me, as I hadn't done it. So all Harrison had to do was to sit tight, and that would be that."

"Moresby always said you were a cool one," Roger wondered. "You certainly are. But you took a big chance. They very nearly did prove it against you, you know. Even now, if Moresby can get hold of any sort of evidence that seems to connect you with Burnt Oak Road, you'll be arrested immediately. And I should say that you'd certainly be convicted."

"But as I've never set foot in the place in my life," returned Wargrave equably, "it's quite impossible for the police to get hold of any such evidence. No, no, I'm safe enough. And so for that matter is Harrison, so long as he doesn't give himself away. There's far less evidence against him than there is against me."

"Yes, that unpardonable carelessness of not unloading or cleaning your revolver, except to wipe his prints off, tells entirely against you. Why did you try to hide it, by the way?"

"Well, wouldn't you have? I can tell you, it came as a nasty shock to me to find that Harrison had even borrowed my revolver to shoot the girl. I never imagined the place would be watched so soon. I was going to throw it into the canal."

"The police would probably have found it there."

"I realise that now. I didn't know then how painstaking they are."

Roger helped himself to more port, and passed the decanter on. "I can't understand why you're taking all this risk and opprobrium to shield that old scoundrel, Wargrave. You're going to marry his daughter, I know, but even then… I mean, you say he's safe from arrest; why not at least let him have the rumours?"

"I wouldn't trust him not to give himself away," Wargrave said seriously. "Rumours soon die down, but it would be the end of the school if its headmaster were actually arrested on a charge of murder. You must see that. Besides," he added perfunctorily, "I expect the girl quite deserved shooting."

Roger marvelled. Wargrave certainly had a practical mind.

"So you not only let the police think what they did, but deliberately encouraged them—for the good of the school?"

"Yes. I worked it all out, and that seemed best. I knew I wasn't in any real danger."

"And you propose to continue on those lines?"

"Certainly. I'm taking it that anything I've said to you this evening has been said in the strictest confidence."

"Oh, absolutely. But it's no breach of confidence for me to go to the police and tell them of the conclusions I'd formed before this evening."

"About Harrison?"

"About Harrison."

Wargrave hesitated. "I'd much prefer that you didn't, Sheringham."

"But what about justice?"

Wargrave shrugged his shoulders.

"And what about your *fiancée*?"

"She doesn't come into it," the other said shortly. "If I

thought it necessary, I could let her know a little. At present she has my word; and she believes it."

"I see. But can you afford the scandal?"

"That will die down."

"I should like to have cleared you," Roger said, almost wistfully.

"Very decent of you. I'd rather you left things."

Roger sipped his port.

"I know," he exclaimed excitedly. "I'll prove that Mary Waterhouse was murdered by one of her old associates, identity unknown, and clear you that way. I can have a lot of fun with that.

"And," he added thoughtfully, "that will be a very nice one back on Moresby."

It was.

THE END

If you've enjoyed *Murder in the Basement*,
you won't want to miss

THESE NAMES MAKE CLUES
by E. C. R. Lorac

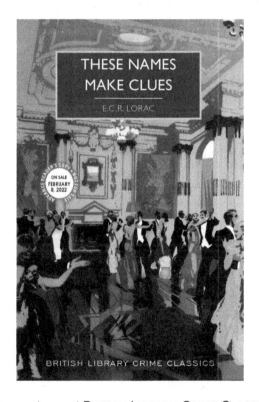

the most recent BRITISH LIBRARY CRIME CLASSIC
published by Poisoned Pen Press,
an imprint of Sourcebooks.

poisonedpenpress.com

Don't miss these favorite British Library Crime Classics available from Poisoned Pen Press!

Mysteries written during the Golden Age of Detective Fiction, beloved by readers and reviewers

Praise for the
British Library Crime Classics

"Carr is at the top of his game in this taut whodunit...The British Library Crime Classics series has unearthed another worthy golden age puzzle."

—Publishers Weekly, STARRED Review,
for *The Lost Gallows*

"A wonderful rediscovery."
—Booklist, STARRED Review, for *The Sussex Downs Murder*

"First-rate mystery and an engrossing view into a vanished world."
—Booklist, STARRED Review, for *Death of an Airman*

"A cunningly concocted locked-room mystery, a staple of Golden Age detective fiction."
—Booklist, STARRED Review, for *Murder of a Lady*

"The book is both utterly of its time and utterly ahead of it."
—New York Times Book Review for *The Notting Hill Mystery*

"As with the best of such compilations, readers of classic mysteries will relish discovering unfamiliar authors, along with old favorites such as Arthur Conan Doyle and G.K. Chesterton."
—Publishers Weekly, STARRED Review, for *Continental Crimes*

"In this imaginative anthology, Edwards—president of Britain's Detection Club—has gathered together overlooked criminous gems."

—Washington Post for *Crimson Snow*

"The degree of suspense Crofts achieves by showing the growing obsession and planning is worthy of Hitchcock. Another first-rate reissue from the British Library Crime Classics series."
—*Booklist*, STARRED Review, for *The 12.30 from Croydon*

"Not only is this a first-rate puzzler, but Crofts's outrage over the financial firm's betrayal of the public trust should resonate with today's readers."
—*Booklist*, STARRED Review, for *Mystery in the Channel*

"This reissue exemplifies the mission of the British Library Crime Classics series in making an outstanding and original mystery accessible to a modern audience."
—*Publishers Weekly*, STARRED Review, for *Excellent Intentions*

"A book to delight every puzzle-suspense enthusiast"
—*New York Times* for *The Colour of Murder*

"Edwards's outstanding third winter-themed anthology show-cases 11 uniformly clever and entertaining stories, mostly from lesser known authors, providing further evidence of the editor's expertise…This entry in the British Library Crime Classics series will be a welcome holiday gift for fans of the golden age of detection."
—*Publishers Weekly*, STARRED Review, for *The Christmas Card Crime and Other Stories*

poisonedpenpress.com